"Mom, please . . . do

"Why not, David?

He clutched her ha
terrible happened to l
something. He got a s on his neck and now . . . now he's not *Dad* anymore! And it got the chief and Officer Kenney, I *know* it did, just now, out there!" His throat began to feel thick and tears stung his eyes. His sweaty palms were sticky against his mom's cool skin as he held her hand in both of his. "Mom, please don't go over the hill, *please!*"

RAY GARTON

Invaders from Mars

Based on the screenplay by Richard Blake

GRAFTON BOOKS
A Division of the Collins Publishing Group

LONDON GLASGOW
TORONTO SYDNEY AUCKLAND

Grafton Books
A Division of the Collins Publishing Group
8 Grafton Street, London W1X 3LA

This novel is a work of fiction. Names, characters, places and incidents are either the product of the author's imagination or are used fictitiously. Any resemblance to actual events or locales or persons, living or dead, is entirely coincidental.

A Grafton UK Paperback Original 1986

First published in the USA by
Pocket Books, a division of Simon & Schuster Inc 1986

ISBN 0-586-07176-8

Printed and bound in Great Britain by
Collins, Glasgow

Set in Times

For:
Tim, Brandee, and Shawn
With love from:
Uncle Ray

Thank you . . .

Scot Holton for countless helpful telephone conversations; Lee Blaine and Mike Mulconnery for patient cooperation; Richard Curtis and Dennis Etchison for some experienced advice; Susan Davis, Mary Papas, and Gina Walworth (who sings beautifully) for all the java.

Invaders from Mars

Chapter One

David Gardiner reached up and grabbed a shirt at random with hardly a glance into his closet, tugged it down from its hanger, and slipped his arms through the short sleeves. As he clumsily buttoned it, he hurried across his bedroom to the fat white and black telescope his dad had given him for his birthday. It was mounted on its stand at David's window, like a soldier at his post, where it seemed to keep watch as David went about his business.

Putting an eye to the scope, David scanned the bright and dewy morning. Birds flitted through blurred branches and fuzzy clouds wandered leisurely across the distant blue. He pulled away a moment to tuck his shirt into his pants, then he peered through the lens again, placed a hand on the side of the scope, moving it down and to the left, creating a swirl of color as it passed rapidly over the trees and brush on Copper Hill. He stopped on the trail and followed it up the hill until it disappeared over the top, then traced it back down again, searching. He scanned the trail a second time, then turned from the telescope to the alarm clock ticking softly on his night stand next to his dumpy little Mr. Potato Head. It was 7:30.

"She's late," David muttered, wondering if she was sick or something.

He went to his dresser, opened a drawer, and removed a fresh pair of socks, then perched on the edge of his unmade bed. Two copies of *Fangoria* magazine, jarred by the sudden movement, slowly slid from the bed onto the floor. The faces of several horror-movie zombies stared up at David from the magazine covers as he put on his socks.

There were magazines and comic books scattered all over the room, sticking out from under the bed, on the windowsill by the telescope, stacked on the desk around his computer, propped against the transparent glass cookie jar that held his penny collection. Behind the computer, against the wall, was a rectangular display case that held David's rock and crystal collection, which included a genuine fossil of a leaf. On a card table between the wall and the end of the desk, a light bulb shined over a terrarium, warming Jasper, the lethargic alligator lizard that lived inside.

The room was cluttered with Godzillas of all sizes, toy spaceships, ray guns, a communicator just like Captain Kirk's, a three-headed rubber snake, a Pinnochio bank, a complete set of *Star Wars* action figures, a cereal bowl full of fake eyeballs. . . .

"How do you *do* it?" Mom often said. "This room was clean two days ago! One of these days, I'll come in here and I won't be able to find you. This stuff is just gonna take over and you'll never be seen again."

But David liked it that way. He enjoyed having all of his things around him, out in the open, visible. He got nervous when they were put away in drawers, in the closet, under the bed. They were too valuable to be hidden—too valuable to him, anyway.

He could hear his mom and dad talking in the kitchen downstairs, their voices muffled by the piercing sounds of the food processor and the orange-juice squeezer. The smell of something cooking drifted into the bedroom through the closed door. It was a dark, burnt smell.

Dad's probably cooking breakfast again, David thought as he tied his shoes.

"Fire!" Mom shrieked, her voice rising easily above the racket of the kitchen appliances.

There was a clatter as Dad bellowed, "Shit!"

"Jesus, George—the *pan!*"

Dad's definitely making breakfast.

David tied his shoes, then bent down and scooped up the fallen magazines, tossing them back onto the bed. As he returned to the telescope, they slid onto the floor again.

Someone turned off the squeezer in the kitchen. Then the food processor was silenced and David could hear his mom's voice, softer now as she spoke to his dad, indecipherable, but with an edge to it.

Then he heard: "David! Get away from that telescope and get *down* here!"

"Yeah, Mom!" he called over his shoulder as he leaned toward the telescope. He passed over the hill a few times, going all the way to the road that curved in front of the house and led into town. Then he swung the scope back to the trail.

He passed over a spot of blue and turned back to

gaze on it. There she was, popping in and out of view behind trees as she jogged along the fence. She became more visible as the greenery thinned out. She was wearing a blue jogging suit that hung loosely on her and was spotted with perspiration. Her forehead glistened with sweat and her eyebrows were bunched together, her face tense, strained. She was moving along at a good pace, her blond hair bouncing on her shoulders, her arms pumping at her sides as she ran.

She was the new school nurse. David didn't know her name yet, but she seemed nice. So much nicer than the last nurse, Mrs. Nivens. She'd been old and hunched, always cranky, as if she needed a nap. This one was younger, pretty, and she always smiled at David when they passed in the hall—even if he didn't smile first! Unlike Mrs. Nivens, who'd always smelled like moldy bread, the new nurse had a warm cinnamony smell about her, sort of like Thanksgiving. It was such a nice smell that whenever he passed her, David slowed down a little to catch it, to enjoy it while it lingered behind her.

She'd only been at the school about two weeks. Apparently she lived nearby because she jogged around the trail on Copper Hill every morning. David hadn't spoken with her yet, and almost wished he'd bang his head on the monkey bars or sprain his ankle playing kickball so he could get the chance. Not that he had anything in particular to say to her; she just seemed so much nicer than most of the grownups at W. C. Menzies Elementary School.

"Sounds like you got a *crush* on her," Doug had told him.

"I do not."

"Sounds like that to *me!*"

Doug was David's best friend, but every once in a while he was a real dork.

The nurse began to disappear behind branches and bushes, her long, tan legs carrying her swiftly and gracefully over the hill. Then she was gone.

"David!" Mom called again. "You'll be late!"

"Okay, okay!"

David moved the telescope across the top of the hill, trying to catch her again, but she was gone.

A flash of yellow! David froze, squinting to see it again. But it wasn't on the hillside. It was on the road, moving toward the house.

His bus.

"Whoa!" he squeaked, jerking his head away from the telescope. David spun around and bounded toward his bed, rolled across the mattress and landed upright on the other side, stumbling toward his desk, toward his penny jar. Perched atop the little mountain of nearly eight hundred pennies was a small felt bag. In it, David kept his rarest, most valuable pennies, and he carried it to school with him every day, just to be on the safe side. David hurriedly reached for the little pouch, wrapped his fingers around it, swiping it away from the top of the other pennies, and knocking the jar over in his rush. The coins rolled and slid across the desktop and spilled over the edge like water over a fall, scattering loudly over the floor, rolling under the bed and night stand, spinning like little tops.

David was so startled by the clamor that he spun around, lifting one arm and hitting his elbow against the display case. The case teetered back and forth a moment, rattling rocks and crystals on their shelves, then it fell forward and clattered onto the desk.

The rocks and pennies clinked together. David, his

eyes still wide from the start he'd gotten, watched as two pennies spun and twirled around a small cylindrical crystal, slower and slower, until they finally collapsed on top of the crystal, as if exhausted.

"What are you *doing* up there?" Mom called. "David?"

He surveyed the mess around him and sighed. It would have to wait until after school. "Coming!" He grabbed his backpack hanging on the back of a chair, and left the room.

Out in the hall, he could hear his parents' voices more clearly.

"They're gonna cut my arm off again!" Dad said.

"Fine, George, as long as they don't cut off your—"

"Ellen, I'm serious."

David's feet clumped down the stairs.

"I thought your design was okay," Mom said. David could hear her distinctive footsteps in the kitchen—light and quick.

"Okay? It's *flawless!* But now they want to cut the payload by 108 kilos. So the first thing they'll do, of course, is slice the bio-lab arm off the probe."

David stepped through the kitchen doorway and turned to his dad, who was at the stove making pancakes. "But, Dad," David said, the bus nearly forgotten now in light of what he'd heard, "the space probe won't work without the arm you designed!"

Dad smiled at him. "Morning, Champ. Yeah, I know it won't."

"So what are you worried about?" Mom asked as she gathered up her books on the kitchen table. She flashed her confidence smile, the one she always gave David when he was worried about an upcoming spelling test or was afraid he was going to botch his lines in a school play. It was warm and bright and seemed to say: *Everything's gonna be fine!*

Dad's worries seemed to fade a bit, if not disappear completely, and he returned the smile. "Who's worried?"

David sprinted over to the refrigerator and took out a can of Dr Pepper, then grabbed a couple of Twinkies from the box on the corner of the counter and stuffed them into his pack.

"Bye!" he chirped, heading out of the kitchen.

"Whoa, Silver!" Mom called. "Wait just a minute."

"But my bus is here, Mom!"

"No, it's not." She moved around behind him and put her hands on his shoulders, steering him over to the table. "Sit down and eat."

As he pulled out a chair, David glanced at the blackened pan lying like a corpse in the sink. It wouldn't be the first time he'd failed to escape one of Dad's breakfasts, and it probably wouldn't be the last time he'd try. Dad could design space probes and shuttles probably better than anybody in the world, David supposed, but he couldn't make a pancake to save his life.

Mom reached into David's pack and pulled out the soda and Twinkies, saying, "Your father has made you a lovely breakfast, David. We don't want it to go to waste." She returned the goodies he'd grabbed.

David looked at his dad, tall and lean with shiny dark hair and tiny soft wrinkles that deepened when he smiled. Pouring batter into a clean pan, Dad said, "Got pancakes, Champ. Your favorite."

David turned to his mom, tried to give her a pleading look, hoping she would say he could go.

Instead, she smiled and said, "Just sit."

The school bus rumbled to a stop out front and honked its horn.

Mom stepped around the table, opened the window, and stuck her head out, waving. "Never mind, Bob!" she yelled. "George will take him today. Thanks!"

"Hey, Dave!" Dad called behind him. "Heads up!"

David turned to see his dad approaching with a plate in one hand and the pan in the other. He set the plate down before David and began waving the pan up and down slightly, smiling with anticipation.

Oh, no, David thought, pressing his back into the chair, *he's gonna try that again.*

Dad flipped the pancake up over the plate and jerked the pan out of the way. The pancake flipped in the air and slapped into David's lap.

Never failed.

David rolled his eyes and groaned, "Dad . . ."

"Good shot!" Mom laughed, gathering her books into her arms.

"No damage done." Dad gingerly lifted the pancake from David's lap and dropped it onto the plate.

"See you guys this afternoon," Mom said. She kissed David on the head.

"Where're *you* going?" David asked.

"I have class."

"But Mom, Dad's made a *lovely* breakfast for you! We don't want it to go to waste!"

"That's right, hon," Dad said solemnly, pouring out another pancake. "Just sit."

Mom looked at them both and sighed, taking a seat across from David. "I'm outnumbered."

David laughed with his dad; they'd won.

"If this course doesn't drive me crazy," Mom said, shoving her books aside, "you two will."

David hitched the strap of the backpack over his shoulder as he followed Dad out the front door to the pickup truck. Mom was backing her car out of the driveway and David waved to her before getting in the pickup.

"George!" she called, sticking her head out the window. "Take him straight to school. He's late already."

"I will, hon. Have a good day!" Dad raised his arm and waved, then got in and started the truck. "Hey, Champ," he said, his voice low, as if Mom might be able to hear, "what do you say we drive by the base. I'll show you the new radar."

"Yeah!" David dropped his pack between his feet and rubbed his hands together, getting that familiar jolt of excitement he always got when he and Dad were alone and doing something fun, something secret, and (more often than not) something Mom had said not to do. Not that David didn't like his mom—he *loved* her. She was a great mom. She was always ready with a big hug; she always spent a lot of time making his Halloween costume every year, which was *always* the best—last year she'd spent weeks making his lizard costume and it looked scarier than anything he could've bought at the store—and she made better potato salad than any of his friends' mothers.

But Dad knew how to have fun! While Mom sometimes objected to David reading "all those violent comic books," Dad *never* missed an issue of *Ironman*. Every Saturday night, David and his dad stayed up to watch Sci-Fi Theater together on channel twelve, and sometimes they even stayed up for the late show if there was a good monster movie scheduled. It was almost as if Dad wasn't a dad at all, but another kid, just like David.

Once David had asked his father why he'd decided to become a NASA engineer.

"So I could play with bigger toys," Dad had said, making those little wrinkles deepen.

Dad always seemed to have a little glimmer in his eyes, like a secret he was keeping just for David. Both Mom and Dad were great parents, but there was something special between David and his dad. Something different.

"The meteor shower's tonight," Dad said.

"That's right!" David turned toward him in the seat. "Can we go outside and watch it?"

"Wouldn't miss it."

David chewed his lip a moment, wondering if he should ask the next question. "Can we stay up late?"

"Well . . . we'll see. You know how your mom is about our bedtimes on weeknights."

"Okay. We'll see." That usually meant that chances were kind of slim.

"Speaking of bedtimes," Dad said, "how're you sleeping?"

"Fine."

"No nightmares?"

"Well . . . once in a while. But not bad," he added quickly, "really." He waited for a response from his dad.

A nod and a smile.

David was relieved. He didn't want to go back to Dr. Wycliffe.

Early last year, David had begun having nightmares. He would wake up screaming almost every night. He usually wouldn't remember the nightmares, but knew they were horrifying.

Mom had told him to stop reading comic books and watching monster movies.

"Don't worry," Dad had said, trying to reassure Mom as much as David. "I used to have nightmares, too. All boys do. Let him have his comics and monsters. The dreams will go away on their own eventually."

When they continued, Mom had insisted that David see a doctor. A psychologist.

"A head doctor!" David had protested, nearly breathless with dread. "A—whatta you call 'em?—a *shrink!* You think I'm crazy!"

"No, no, Champ," Dad had said softly, putting his arm around David. "We don't think you're crazy. Mom just thinks . . . *we* think that it might be a good idea for you to see this doctor. Maybe he can find out why you're having nightmares and help you get rid of them. Remember when Dr. Stewart took your tonsils out to get rid of that awful sore throat? It's sort of like that."

But it *hadn't* been like that. Dr. Stewart was a pleasant man with silver hair who gave his patients chewing gum before they left the office.

Dr. Wycliffe had been short and fat with a pinched voice. The first thing David had noticed about him was his hair. There had been something odd about it. On his third and last visit to Wycliffe, he figured out what it was: the hair wasn't real! It was a wig! A "too-pay," Dad had called it. David decided that any guy who'd wear a wig had to be pretty loopy. Besides that, he couldn't stand Dr. Wycliffe's squeaky voice and the way he was constantly flicking his pudgy little nose with his finger, as if it were always itching.

Dad had talked it over with Mom and they'd decided that David wouldn't have to go back to Dr. Wycliffe if he really didn't want to. Maybe the nightmares would go away.

They did, eventually, just as Dad had said they would. But David still had one now and then. Sometimes he dreamed about Dr. Wycliffe's "too-pay": a black, furry animal squatting on the fat man's head.

David leaned forward in the seat as they approached the marine base. It was set a short distance off the road, surrounded by a tall chain-link fence with barbed wire around the top. At the front entrance, uniformed guards stood around what looked like the box office at the Sky-Vu Drive-in and a large sign hung over the gate. It read in bold letters:

U.S. MARINE CORPS BASE
CAMP LEWIS B. PULLER
CALIFORNIA

"Can we go in, Dad?"

"Uh-uh."

"C'mon, just for a minute? We've come *this* far."

"Not today. We're late already. You want us to get caught playing hooky?"

David squinted at him. "*Hooky?* You mean cuttin' class, Dad. Nobody says *hooky* anymore."

"Whatever. They've probably got bloodhounds searching for you right now, sniffing at your dirty old sweat socks."

David laughed and punched his dad's shoulder.

Then he spotted the radar and leaned forward again, putting his hands on the dashboard. "There!" he exclaimed, pointing. "That's it, isn't it?"

Within the compound, two large radar dishes slowly and diligently swept back and forth, scanning the sky.

"Yep," Dad said. "They're fully operational now."

"How does it work?"

"Okay, see, it's a phased-array system," he explained, hunkering forward over the steering wheel, as if he were leaning over a campfire to tell a story. "A short pulse of energy is transmitted into the sky, and if something's out there, the energy is reflected back and detected on a sensitive receiver."

As Dad drove slowly by, David watched the two radar dishes, his lower lip tucked between his teeth. He tried to imagine what those energy pulses would look like if he could see them as they shot into the sky—like big, glowing candy bars? Like bolts of lightning?—and he tried to imagine them bouncing off the side of an enemy jet or . . . or maybe even an alien spaceship, zooming back to earth like high-tech Paul Reveres with a message of impending danger.

Two jets roared by overhead, flying low and breaking through David's daydream.

"What if the energy pulses missed, Dad?" David asked.

He shook his head. "If something's out there, they'll find it."

David turned around in the seat and got on his knees, watching the dishes grow smaller as they drove on.

"What if they didn't come back?"

Dad thought about that a moment, then said slowly, "Well, then, I guess we'd have to put an ad in the paper offering a reward to anyone who finds and returns some lost energy pulses."

For a moment, David thought his dad was serious; then he saw the crooked smile and laughed, turning back around in the seat.

"You sure we can't go in for just a minute, Dad?" he asked.

"Positive. But . . ." Dad paused, looking at David from the corner of his eye. ". . . if you want, you can steer until we get to the main road."

"Okay!"

They scooted the bench seat back a notch and David squirmed onto his dad's lap. He put a hand on each side of the wheel.

"Eyes on the road," Dad said, his voice soft.

"Eyes on the road," David echoed.

Dad wrapped his arms around David's waist and gave him a warm squeeze.

Chapter Two

The halls were deserted when David got to school. The door to every classroom was shut tight and all the classes were in progress.

Mrs. McKeltch is gonna be pissed, David thought as he began to run. Mrs. McKeltch was always pissed, it seemed, and usually at something David had done—sometimes even if he hadn't done anything.

Mrs. McKeltch was his homeroom teacher this year. Last year she'd just been a matronly woman with tightly curled and wavy gray hair. He'd seen her walking very fast through the halls in her stuffy old-lady dresses that always smelled like mothballs. They were always black or gray or brown with lots of busy swirls and curly-cues and stripes, and they always came below her knees. Her stockings were usually wrinkled slightly from her knees all the way to her thick ankles where they seemed to be stuffed into the flat, black shoes she always wore. Her shoes were almost totally silent as she stormed through the halls, her big hands curled into fists that weren't quite clenched at her sides, looking as if she were on her way to the principal's office, anxious to have some poor student expelled from school. She'd never smiled at David nor spoken to him—she hadn't even seemed to notice him, in fact.

She noticed him *this* year, though, and, as far as David could tell, she didn't like him. Didn't like him at *all*. Now when he saw her storming down the hall, it seemed she was hurrying to the principal's office to expel *him*.

The thought of Mrs. McKeltch—the way her jaw always jutted and her eyes narrowed to little cuts in her puffy face when she was angry, the way she always seemed to be thinking silently, *This is the last straw!*—made David run faster. His backpack jostled at his side and he clutched his pouch of pennies in his right hand. His feet made thunderous echoes in the empty halls as he rounded a corner and smacked into somebody hurrying in the other direction. David fell on his behind and his pennies spilled from the felt bag, jingling over the hall floor in a shower of copper. He locked his elbows and propped himself up on both hands, his legs splayed before him.

It was the nurse.

She was getting to her feet when David looked up, brushing off her burgundy skirt and running a hand through her blond hair.

"Are you all right?" she asked with a breathy laugh.

"Yeah, I'm okay." He didn't know what to do first—stand or start picking up pennies.

"Let me help you," she said, reaching out her hand.

David took it and pulled himself up. Her hand was

smooth and cool. He smelled her perfume then, that cinnamony holiday smell. The blue name tag on her coat read: LINDA MAGNUSON, R.N.

She bent down and quickly began picking up pennies. "You sure have a lot of pennies," she said.

"Yeah. I have over 760." David started picking them up, too, noticing that some had rolled way down the hall. He would just have to let them go; he had to get to class.

"Looks like you're a little late," Linda said, getting down on her knees to make the job a little easier.

"Yeah."

"Me, too." She laughed again; she had a pretty laugh. "I got lost this morning jogging in the hills by my house. I took a different path today and it took me nearly forty minutes to find my way back home!" She shook her head, embarrassed at herself.

David stopped a smile at her. "Yeah, I saw you," he said, instantly regretting his words. *That was stupid,* he thought. *Now she'll think I'm some kinda perv! A peeping tom!*

She cocked a brow as she held out a handful of pennies, giving him a quizzical smirk. "You did, huh?"

David opened the pouch and she dropped in the coins. "Through my telescope," he added. "I have a . . . a telescope in my bedroom window." *Dumber and dumber,* he thought, embarrassed. "I live just over the hill from you. I think."

She picked up some more of the coins. "Do you always watch people through your telescope?"

"No. Usually just stars. At night, I mean. Tonight there's gonna be a meteor shower."

"Really?"

"Yeah. My dad and me are gonna watch it." He couldn't hide the anticipation in his voice.

"Here." She handed him the last of the pennies and stood, brushing off her knees. Leaning toward him conspiratorially, she whispered, "Don't let the hall monitor catch you." She waggled her fingers at him as she started to walk away. "Enjoy the meteors."

David headed for his classroom, stuffing the pouch into his backpack. Impulsively, he spun around and said with a smile, "You smell nice!" Then, before she could look back, he turned away, giggling into his palm.

Linda Magnuson was still smiling when she got to her office. The boy reminded her of the crush she'd had on her fifth-grade teacher, Mr. Scribner. He'd been a tall man with thick dark hair and a craggy face. Had it been possible, she would've watched *him* through a telescope, too. She wondered if the boy's parents knew he was standing at his window spying on the school nurse in the mornings. Oh, well, it happened to everybody at that age, and usually more than once, before adolescence. Before that sort of thing got complicated and painful. The boy was at least normal, which was more than she could say for a few of the staff members at W. C. Menzies Elementary School.

Mr. Cross, the principal, was a nice enough man, but during the short time Linda had been at the school, she had yet to see a single sign of leadership in the man. He was tall, thin, and bald, walked with a bit of a hunch in his back, as if to compensate for his height, and seemed more eager to please everyone than to run the school responsibly. His attempts to welcome her and settle her into the routine at W. C. Menzies were comical. For the first week, he was always poking his head into her office and saying, "Hi-de-hi! How are we getting along?" His intentions were good, she was sure, but rather annoying.

Linda seated herself at her desk and found a note written in small, economical handwriting.

Ms. Magnuson:

Sorry to see you were unable to make this morning's faculty meeting.

—Mrs. McKeltch

"Yeah, I'll bet you were," Linda muttered, crumpling the note up in her fist and tossing it into the trash can.

McKeltch was another odd duck. *Crimson bitch is more like it,* Linda thought, slipping off her coat and hanging it on the back of her chair.

Mrs. McKeltch seemed to be the one who ran the school. She'd been there longer than anyone and seemed to be the type who would stay until she dropped dead. Stuffy and unpleasant, neither smiling nor expressing any feeling other than, perhaps, silently boiling contempt for everyone and everything around her, Mrs. McKeltch stalked the halls like a warden in a low-budget women's prison movie. Linda supposed she ran her classes the same way, and she pitied the woman's students.

From what little Linda had heard about her—and it was very little since the other faculty members did not speak of her often, and even then in hushed, fearful tones with cautious glances left and right—Mrs. McKeltch had been married briefly, many years ago, to the local librarian, a timid little man who, only a few months later, left town suddenly, leaving behind an unattended library and an unfazed wife. No one knew if the divorce had ever been made official, although it probably didn't matter because Mr. McKeltch had never been seen or heard from again. Some joked that she'd murdered him and buried him in her fruit cellar, but everyone knew better. No one in his right mind would have stuck around long enough for that to happen and, although Mr. McKeltch had been timid, he was said to have been very smart and resourceful. He'd got away while the getting was good.

There were rumors, of course, about Mrs. McKeltch's sexual preference. Linda tried, as a rule, to disregard hearsay about anyone, but that possibility had occurred to Linda the day she'd arrived at Menzies. Mrs. McKeltch had stepped before her in the hall, apparently from nowhere.

"Well," Mrs. McKeltch had said, "you must be the new nurse."

"Yes. Linda Magnuson."

"Mrs. McKeltch. Welcome. You'll have plenty to keep you busy here. You know how clumsy and irresponsible children are. Always hurting themselves one way or another. Of course, they're just after our attention, but—" A tight smile, there and gone. "—what are we to do? Well," she'd said, cocking a brow and looking Linda up and down slowly—a bit *too* slowly for Linda's comfort, "I'll be seeing you around, I'm sure." Then she'd strutted off prissily, her dark, matronly dress fluttering about her.

Linda sighed heavily, pushing Mrs. McKeltch from her mind. Time to get to work.

* * *

David stood in front of the classroom door, staring up at the strip of green plastic that read: MRS. MCKELTCH—5TH GRADE. He could hear a man's voice inside.

Turning the doorknob slowly, quietly, he opened the door just a crack and peered into the classroom. Two uniformed men stood before the students. David recognized them both from the base. One was General Wilson—Dad called him Mad Dog Wilson, always saying the name with a laugh—and beside him stood Captain Rinaldi.

"Camp Puller is where we train one of the Marine Corps' largest air-to-ground combat teams," General Wilson was saying, his hands joined behind him, his feet spread, as if he were standing at ease. He was a tall man with gray hair, a craggy face, and just a bit of a paunch above his belt. "Our infantry and aviation forces can respond to threats from *any* enemy force," he went on, sounding just a bit nervous. He and Captain Rinaldi came to the school once every year to talk about the base and to invite the teachers and their students to come visit, and every year there was a field trip to the base, always led by General Wilson. He would always seem slightly uncomfortable, though, as if he weren't quite sure how to act around so many kids.

David opened the door a little farther and poked his head in, looking around for Mrs. McKeltch. She was to the right of the door, looking stern as always, her eyes scanning the students, looking for misbehavior of any kind, like those two radar dishes watching the skies for . . . whatever.

Heather turned to the door, saw David, and smiled,

shaking her blond head slowly, as if to say, "Shame on you."

Mrs. McKeltch saw the girl turn, followed her gaze, and spotted David. She turned her whole body to him, clenching her fists for an instant. *"David Gardiner!"* she hissed. She sounded like Jasper when she talked that way; the lizard always hissed when he was angry or scared.

"Sorry," David whispered, stepping inside and closing the door softly.

"This is the third time this month," she said, hissing again, stepping toward him and leaning forward, her head cocked a bit, her eyes narrow with anger.

Every head in the room turned to David, and he felt his face getting warm as he made his way to his desk. He was just two rows up from the door, but with all those eyes trained on him, it felt like a mile.

Before he could get to his seat, Doug grabbed David's hand as he walked by, pressing a tightly folded note into his palm. David wrapped his fingers around it and sat down, hanging his backpack over the back of his seat.

"I'm sorry, General Wilson," Mrs. McKeltch said. "Please go ahead."

General Wilson fidgeted, cleared his throat, and glanced at Captain Rinaldi, who smirked at Wilson's discomfort, casually trying to hide his amusement behind the knuckles of his right hand, moving them across his lips.

"Thank you," General Wilson said, nodding to Mrs. McKeltch. "Um, we at Camp Puller are your protection against any hostile forces that threaten the peace and security of this school, city, or the country."

David turned to Heather, who was seated next to

him. She was still smiling. David shrugged one shoulder, then looked down at the note. It was folded into a tiny square. He opened it slowly, trying not to let the paper crinkle.

LATE AGAIN,
DICK BRAIN!

David looked at Doug, grinning at David with his head in his hands, elbows on his desktop, and smiled. Doug was always writing him notes like that, calling him names—usually dirty ones that would curl any parent's hair—but it was okay, because they were friends.

A hand shot over David's shoulder and grabbed the note, tearing it away from him suddenly. David turned around to see Kevin Addams reading it, hunched over in his desk behind David.

"Gimme that!" David snapped, instantly wishing he hadn't.

"*Mis*ter Gardiner!" Mrs. McKeltch hissed.

He looked to the back of the room and saw her glaring at him, her jaw jutting.

"I want to see you after class today," she said, the hiss gone, her voice suddenly low and level with anger.

David slumped in his desk, feeling the eyes of the whole class on him again. Snickers and chuckles rose from the students.

"*Quiet!*" Mrs. McKeltch demanded, moving to the center of the classroom. She held up her hand, a gesture with which the entire class was familiar, and chanted, "*One*, two, *three*, four, *five!*"

Instant silence. It always worked. On the first day of

class, Mrs. McKeltch had told them, "When I do this—" She'd held up her hand and counted to five in a stern, singsong fashion. "—I want silence. Anyone still talking or causing a disturbance by the time I reach five will be punished." She'd never had to repeat the rule.

Mrs. McKeltch pressed her hands together before her and smiled—at least, it was a smile for Mrs. McKeltch: a tight twitching of her lips—nodding to General Wilson.

"I'm sorry, General," she said. "Go on."

General Wilson fidgeted some more, cleared his throat again, then leaned back against the chalk tray below the blackboard.

"Well," he said, "any questions?"

"Yes," Kevin said. "Is everybody on the base a Marine?"

He's such a smartass, David thought.

"Well, um," General Wilson replied, scratching his chin, "they usually are on a Marine base."

David sneaked a look over his shoulder and scowled at Kevin, who grinned back coldly.

The class laughed at General Wilson's reply, and Wilson didn't seem to know quite how to take it. He straightened his tie and pursed his lips a few times.

Captain Rinaldi was obviously enjoying himself. He leaned his back against the wall to General Wilson's left, smiling at the general's nervousness, folding his arms across his chest.

"Um, actually," General Wilson went on, "Camp Puller is a little special. We have a research facility there, operated by NASA, which is part of their space program. So, aside from just Marines, we have a number of scientists, engineers, and technicians."

"Any astronauts?" Cindy Potter asked.

General Wilson smiled at her and shrugged. "Once in a while an astronaut passes through." He pointed to Scot. "Yes, another question?"

"How do you keep track of things in space when you can't see 'em from down here?" Scot asked.

"We have a brand-new radar that can pick up anything that moves across the sky, day or night," General Wilson answered.

"That's the phased-array system," David interjected without giving it a thought. He tensed, awaiting another scolding from Mrs. McKeltch. Instead, the general smiled broadly at him.

"That's right, David." He addressed the entire class then: "As some of you may know, David's father works in Puller's research facility and has been a big part of some of our most important projects." He turned to David again. "Do you know how the phased array system works, David?"

"Yes, sir."

"Why don't you explain it to the class?"

"Well, see, it's . . ." All eyes were on him again, but this time they were attentive, interested. ". . . it's where energy pulses are shot into the sky, and if there's anything out there, the energy bounces off of it and comes back. Then it's picked up by a receiver." He chewed on his lip a moment, looking at General Wilson. "Is that right?"

The general nodded. "Very good, David, that's exactly right."

David couldn't resist a glance at Mrs. McKeltch, a proud smile, letting her know that not everything he said was just a classroom disturbance.

She simply glared back.

"I'd like to welcome all of you to the base," General Wilson said. "Captain Rinaldi and I would be happy to give you a tour and answer any questions you have." He turned to Mrs. McKeltch. "You can call me personally and arrange a visit almost any time."

"Thank you, General."

"Well, boys and girls, I hope you have a better idea of what we're doing at Camp Puller. I've enjoyed talking to you today and I hope you'll look at me—"

The bell rang and David's stomach did a little flip. That meant he'd be talking with Mrs. McKeltch soon.

"—and the other Marines on the base as your friends."

The students applauded as they stood and gathered their things. Kevin Addams applauded, as usual.

David stood, swinging his bag over his shoulder. Maybe there was a chance he could slip out before Mrs. McKeltch caught him. He turned and found her standing just inches in front of him, looking down her nose through slitted eyes.

She suddenly smiled over David's head and he turned to see General Wilson and Captain Rinaldi approaching.

"How'd I do?" Wilson asked Rinaldi quietly.

Rinaldi held his hand out, palm down, and tilted it back and forth, chuckling.

"Thank you for coming," Mrs. McKeltch said with a wide smile. "My students always enjoy your visits."

"Our pleasure, Mrs. McKletch," Wilson said.

Mrs. McKeltch's smile faltered, and she suddenly looked forced. "McKeltch," she said stiffly, almost under her breath.

"General Wilson," David said.

"Yes, David?"

"You guys aren't gonna cut off my dad's arm, are you?"

General Wilson blinked rapidly several times and his mouth opened as if to speak, but he said nothing for a moment. Then he said, "Excuse me?"

"The arm on the space probe. Dad said you might have to cut it off."

Wilson's face relaxed; he looked relieved.

"The probe won't work without the arm, General."

"I haven't heard anything about that, David," Wilson said, smiling. "I promise I'll look into it."

"Thank you, sir."

Before leaving, the general winked at Mrs. McKeltch and said, "Don't be too hard on him."

After the two men left, the room became smotheringly silent. Mrs. McKeltch folded her arms before her chest and jutted her jaw.

"This is the third time in one month that you've been late to class, Mr. Gardiner," she said softly, but not without threat. "And it's certainly not the first time you've disrupted the class."

"But Kevin was the one who—" David began.

"Don't try to shift the blame to someone *else*, Mr. Gardiner. I don't want to hear it."

His mouth shut with an audible clap.

Mrs. McKeltch stared at him thoughtfully for a moment, one finger tapping her arm. "What am I going to do with you?" She slowly walked a circle around him, looking him up and down, as if she were going to make a purchase. "Should I have a talk with your parents? They wouldn't be at all pleased. They're on *my* side, you know. Parents always are." She stopped behind him.

David felt a wave of paranoia wash over him. It was

like having his back turned on a vicious, barking dog. But for some reason, he was afraid to turn around and face her.

"Do you suppose that General Wilson was always in trouble when *he* was in school? Of course not. He did not get to be such an important man by being a nuisance. He followed the rules. He behaved. Keep that in mind, David Gardiner, the next time you dawdle on your way to class or want to pass a note to another student. If you don't shape up, you'll go nowhere, do you understand me, young man? You'll never amount to the likes of General Wilson." She stepped forward and bent down, making her face grow; it loomed before David's eyes like a moon. She added quietly, "You'll never amount to *anything* if you don't behave."

David watched her mouth as she spoke, noticing how fast her lips moved over her cigarette-yellowed teeth, opening and closing, squirming like two worms.

"Well," she said, standing straight, checking her watch, "I have to drive to Copper Hill and collect frogs for tomorrow's dissection. Go on now, before you're late for your *next* class."

"Yes, ma'am," David said, hurrying to the door.

"But—"

David stopped and turned to her again.

"Don't let it happen again."

"I won't."

He walked calmly out of the room, then broke into a run just outside the door. The crowded hall had never looked so good.

On the way home, David sat with Doug near the back of the bus. The rumble of the engine mixed with the laughter and chatter of young voices, filling the bus with a low roar.

"So," Doug said, toying with a green rubber band, "did Mrs. McKeltch chew your butt, or what?"

"Yeah, she chewed it all right." David watched as Doug bent down and swept his hand over the floor. He came up with a pebble between his thumb and forefinger. "I don't know what I ever did to make her pick on me like she does," David said glumly.

"She's gotta pick on somebody. Might as well be you." Doug laughed, fashioning the rubber band into a little slingshot and loading it with the pebble. He looked around for a target and smiled when his gaze stopped on Mr. Bob, the bus driver.

Mr. Bob (nobody knew his last name) overflowed in his seat, he was so big. There was only a little reddish hair on the sides of his head; the top and back were mostly bald. Little folds of fat gathered at the back of his neck.

Doug tossed a devilish glance at David, aimed, and shot the pebble to the front of the bus.

It smacked the back of Mr. Bob's neck and bounced off. His meaty hand slapped over the spot and the bus swerved a little, making the kids sway back and forth in their seats. Mr. Bob yelled something that was lost in all the noise.

When he pulled his hand away, there was a small cut on his neck, bleeding just a bit.

Doug grinned at David. "Pretty good shot, huh?"

The boys laughed.

Chapter Three

When David walked into the house, his mom was just hanging up the phone.

"That was your dad," she said. "He's going to be a little late this evening."

"How late?" David asked, a hint of panic in his voice.

"Not too late to watch the meteor shower with you. He wanted me to be sure and tell you that."

"Oh. Good." David followed her into the kitchen. "I'm hungry." He grabbed an orange from the bowl on the table and began to peel it clumsily. "How'd your class go today?"

"I had a test."

"Did you flunk?"

"Of course I didn't *flunk*, silly," she said with a smile, knowing that David was only joking. She opened the dishwasher and began to load it with the mess left from breakfast. "I *studied.* You should follow your mother's example."

David took a seat at the table. "Did you write little notes on your fingers and palms before you went into class?" he asked, trying to conceal his grin.

"Perish the thought! That would be cheating. Your mother does not cheat. I studied and I think I did very well. I might have missed a couple questions, but overall, it was a success."

Pulling the orange apart, David took a bite of a juicy wedge and chewed hungrily. "I still can't figure out why—"

"Don't talk with your mouth full."

He swallowed and wiped his mouth. "I still can't figure out why you go to school when you don't *have* to anymore."

"To learn. I wanted to learn how to keep our books better, so I took a home-economics course. If I wanted to learn how to cook French food, I'd take a French-cooking course. At your age, kids go to school because they *have* to, so they can learn the things they'll need to know when they grow up. Adults go to school to improve upon what they already know. Sort of like reading a book to learn something, only you're getting it from a teacher."

"Then you don't have to go to school—I've got *lots* of books you can read."

"I said *improve*, not *derange*," she said and laughed. "How was your day?"

"Mrs. McKeltch chewed my—I mean, she kept me after class again. 'Cause I was late."

"She did, huh? Well, then we'll just have to try a little harder to get you to class on time."

"She'd do it anyway. She doesn't like me."

Mom turned to him and leaned on the dishwasher. "Why do you say that?"

"Well . . . sometimes it seems like she enjoys it when I do something she can rag me about. She's just . . ." He thought a moment, then shrugged. ". . . mean, I guess. She likes to get kids in trouble I think."

"That's not the right attitude for a teacher to have," Mom said, closing the dishwasher and adjusting the dial.

"She says you're on her side."

"Oh, she *does*, huh?" Mom came over and took a wedge from his orange, popping it into her mouth. "Well, maybe I'll have to talk to *her* after school someday and tell her otherwise."

David laughed. "Don't talk with your mouth full, Mom," he said.

Mom tousled his hair as she chewed the orange. "Smartass."

Before David could get out of the house, his mom told him that if he had any homework, he should get to it early so he could watch the meteor shower that night. He went upstairs and cleaned up the spilled rocks and pennies, then worked for a while on a history book report. When he was finished, he changed his clothes and got his battery-operated Godzilla from a shelf. Gathering up his toy cars and the little skyscrapers he'd made from cardboard and egg cartons, he went down to the sand pit.

Godzilla had destroyed the doomed city half a dozen times, his shadow lengthening in the dying sunlight, before David heard the distant sound of his dad's car driving up over the hill. As he lay on his stomach in the warm sand, watching the monster walk on another building with his fanged mouth opening and closing, David heard the car door slam. He waited several minutes before Dad's footsteps began crunching and scuffing over the hill.

"Hey, Champ!" Dad called, appearing on the trail. He stopped at the drop-off, hands in pockets.

"What's doin'?" he asked with a grin.

"I'm trashing Tokyo."

"A dirty job, but somebody's gotta do it. Have a good day?"

"Yeah, it was okay. Mr. Bob swerved the bus all over the place coming home."

"He *did?* What happened?"

"Doug shot him in the back of the neck with a little rock."

Dad stifled a snicker.

David smirked, half at the memory, half at his dad's reaction. "It made a little cut right here—" He touched the back of his neck. "—on one of those little fat rolls."

Although he never said anything in front of Mom (she didn't like him to "set a bad example"), Dad had once told David he thought Bob was a slob—"Bob the slob!" they'd laughed—who looked more like a bus than a bus driver.

Dad cleared his throat and swallowed his laughter. "That wasn't very nice."

Godzilla tripped on a toy Jeep and fell on his face, taking out a quarter of the city. His legs continued to walk as he rocked back and forth, eating sand.

"Why don't you bring Tokyo back to the house. Dinner's almost ready." He started back over the hill.

David turned off Godzilla, got on his knees and started to gather up the city and cars. He tried to get up, but fell forward. Something was holding his left foot.

David froze, clutching the buildings and cars to his chest. He tugged his foot again, but couldn't pull it away. The toys slid from his arms and quietly scattered on the sand. David's mouth was suddenly dry and hanging open, his breath drawing in and out a bit faster. He could feel pressure on each side of his foot. He pulled one more time, weakly, but it wouldn't let go.

Images began to form in his mind: a hand? A claw reaching out of the smooth white sand?

Adrenaline surged through David and a sudden chill blanketed his whole body as he watched his dad disappear over the crest of Copper Hill.

Something green, maybe? Something with scales and talons? Something very strong that might begin to pull him, drag him down into the sand? Something that might, at that very moment, be rising out of the sand behind him, reaching for his back with its other claw? He couldn't bring himself to look over his shoulder.

A whimper quivered from David and turned into a scream as he tore himself away and frantically crawled across the sand. *"Dad!"* He kicked up sand as he got to his feet and ran, stumbling across the pit toward the trail, shimmying up the incline to Dad, who was already hurrying back over the hill. "Dad!" David gasped, grabbing his dad's hand and pulling him down the drop-off and onto the sand, pointing.

"What, Champ? What is it?" Dad asked, startled by David's outburst.

"Some—something in the—" David stopped, staring at the spot where he'd been playing. The toys were scattered over the sand. A few feet from them, a half-buried branch stuck out of the white sand, one forked end lying where David's foot had been.

The fear subsided rapidly and David lowered his arm, his mouth still open. It had just been a branch caught on his sneaker. He looked up at his dad, who was still anxiously awaiting an explanation.

David remembered something that Dr. Wycliffe had asked: "David, do you ever imagine things when you're awake? Things that don't seem like a nightmare, but seem *real?* It's important that you tell me so I can help you." He remembered the doctor's "toopay," his squeaky voice, and snapped his mouth shut, blinking a few times. He didn't want Dr. Wycliffe's help, and if Dad thought he was having nightmares while he was *awake*, he just might have to go back to that fat little man behind the big desk.

Swallowing hard, David said, "Nothing, Dad. I guess it was nothing."

Dad looked from David to the branch, then back to David again, smiling. He seemed to know then what had happened and he squeezed David's shoulder.

"Okay, Champ. If you say so. C'mon back to the house now."

"Yeah, I'm coming." David went back to his toys and slowly began to pick them up again, keeping an eye on the branch.

Must've been buried in the sand, he thought, *and my foot pulled it out.*

It certainly looked like a claw with bony, crooked fingers, slowly rising from the sand, ready to grab and hold whatever or whoever might be in reach.

Only a branch, he said to himself silently.

Just the same, he kept his distance.

The night settled slowly and comfortably over David's house and yard, over the quiet hill in back. There was no breeze to stir the scrub pines into which the crooked trail disappeared, and they remained perfectly still, standing like guards over the hill's surroundings.

The peacefulness was suddenly broken by the hollow, metallic scream of the back screen door as David and his dad came out into the back yard. They'd turned out all the back lights so the yard was dark. They went around to the side of the house that was darkest and looked upward.

The night sky was filled with Christmas; the stars sparkled like silver glitter scattered by God and the moon hovered among them like a great radiant snowball.

Hidden by the cover of night, crickets chirped and frogs croaked.

Dad touched David's shoulder. "C'mon," he whispered. It was a night for whispers.

They moved over to the bench that Dad had built for just such occasions—they called it their "night bench"—and lay on it like stacked wood, their heads together, gazing upward.

"There!" David exclaimed, pointing at a bright spot of light shooting across the sky. "Wow, a fireball!"

"Bright one, too."

It arced gracefully, then disappeared, as if it had never been.

David snuggled closer to his dad. "Look," he said quietly, "there's Mars. See? Right over there."

Dad followed the direction of David's finger and spotted the planet, shining brightly against the black velvet of night.

"It's pretty close," he said.

"Yeah, it's at the perihelion right now. It's only 30 million miles from Earth."

"Only 30 million," Dad said. "No wonder it looks so close."

David turned to see Dad smirking at him. "Cut it out, Dad." He laughed, punching him lovingly on the shoulder.

An owl hooted from the trees on the hill and from the distance, the lonely call of a whippoorwill sounded.

Three meteorites cut across the sky like missiles, almost as fast as a blink.

"Here they come," David said, almost reverently.

After a few moments, they began coming in heavily, one every few seconds, a silent, graceful ballet of light. The meteorites arced before the still, watchful stars, shooting downward to the earth to meet a fiery end.

"There's more this year than last," David said, never turning his eyes from the sky.

"Looks like the heaviest shower of the year."

The owl hooted again as more meteorites burned through the night.

"Mom's missing a good show," David said with a smile. They'd left her in the house on the phone, talking to one of her classmates about the day's test.

For a few moments, the sky was inactive. The stars continued to glimmer, as if waiting, along with David and his dad, for more. The peace was broken by what began as a tiny flicker. It quickly grew brighter and brighter, grew bigger as it plummeted out of the sky. Its light became so bright that it illuminated the whole back yard like a floodlight.

"Holy *shit!*" David shouted, jumping to his feet.

Dad got up beside him, gawking upward with his jaw slack. "Jesus, that's bright!" he breathed.

The huge meteorite moved like a living thing across the sky, pulling its long, diminishing tail behind as it flew. It brought with it a faint, distant rumbling sound, like thunder, but more intense, more explosive.

"Hear it?" Dad asked.

"Yeah!" David gasped, his face glowing in the light from the sky. "That one's *not* gonna vaporize! It's gonna make it through the atmosphere!"

"It's got a hell of a tail!"

Its brightness grew into a cool, shimmering ball of white. The sound rumbled louder, building to a crescendo. Then it faded and was gone. The back yard was dark once again. The sky was still. A few small pinpoints of light shot from one end of the sky to the other, hardly visible compared to the monstrous meteorite that had just disappeared.

David and his dad remained still as stone for a moment, their eyes glued to the sky, their mouths open in awe, their arms held tensely a few inches out from their sides. Then they lowered their eyes and looked at one another, smiling, enchanted, silently sharing the magic of what they'd just seen.

* * *

Ellen Gardiner stood at the back door and watched her husband and son through the screen, her arms folded over her breasts, a loving smile playing on her lips. After hanging up the phone, she'd intended to go outside and watch the shower with them, but she'd decided not to break the spell between them.

David was definitely his father's boy. Their relationship often seemed more like that of two playmates rather than a father and his son. Sometimes, just sometimes, deep inside, Ellen felt a pang of sadness that her relationship with David wasn't more like George's. It wasn't jealousy, really—more like a kind of regret mixed, perhaps, with just a pinch of envy. She often thought, however, that maybe it was better that way. Sometimes it seemed that George and David were almost *too* close; perhaps there wasn't enough distance for George to notice when something wasn't right. *Someone* had to keep a level head, a watchful eye.

Like last year when David was having those nightmares. Ellen had been worried for a while, thinking that perhaps she and George were doing something wrong, that they were somehow responsible for whatever was bothering David. She'd quickly changed her mind, however, after looking through all the comic books and magazines David read. They were filled with such horrible stories! They even made her—an adult who should know better—squirm. And the magazines contained stills from horror movies that looked more like photographs from a coroner's files: spears through heads, throats slashed open, entrails dangling from sliced-open abdomens. She'd been appalled and had insisted he stop reading them. George had protested, though, saying he'd had similar tastes as a boy. So they compromised: Dr. Wycliffe. When it became apparent he wasn't helping, David had stopped seeing him. Fortunately, the nightmares had gone away. But Ellen *still* wished he wouldn't read that trash. And if the nightmares returned, she wouldn't hesitate to be firm about changing David's reading material. No matter what George said. Whatever happened to Nancy Drew and the Hardy Boys?

Oh well, she thought, *he gets good grades, he's bright and healthy. It could be worse.*

She watched with a smile as they marveled at an unusually bright meteorite, standing and pointing at it excitedly. She saw its light, but never took her eyes from them. The love between the two of them was far more spectacular than any meteor shower. When she thought of some of her friends—the problems they had with their children, the bitterness in their homes—she thanked God, or whatever was out there, for what she had. She wouldn't change it, or let it be changed, for all the wealth and fame in the world.

She pushed the screen door open and it screeched loudly, catching their attention. They turned to her and smiled. George waved and David began hopping excitedly from one foot to the other.

"Mom!" he shouted. "You *missed* it!"

"I saw it from the back door," she said.

George swept his fingers through his hair, shaking his head. "God, it was incredible, Ellen."

"Time to go to bed, David," she said gently, knowing he wouldn't like it.

"But it just started, Mom!"

"I know, but you have school tomorrow."

"So do you."

"That's why," she said, putting an arm around him, "we're *all* going to bed."

George joined his hands behind his back and looked up at the sky. "Not me!" he said with conviction.

David stood firmly next to his father. "Me neither!"

Ellen laughed and took his hand. "We'll see about that."

Mom pulled the covers up to David's neck, tugging them over his shoulders a little, making him cozy and warm.

"How do you think I'm ever gonna become an astronaut if you won't let me stay up late?" David asked her, still put out at having to come inside and go to bed.

"Astronauts need sleep just like everyone else," she replied, leaning down and kissing him.

Dad perched himself on the foot of the bed, a copy of *Fantascene* magazine open on his lap, his forehead tense as he read.

"Did you finish all your homework?" Mom asked.

"Did you finish *yours?*" David asked, squirming under the blankets.

Mom made her fingers into claws and began tickling David's ribs over the covers. "*Yes,* I finished it, smart aleck!" she growled. Then she gently put a hand on the side of his smiling face and said, "Now go to sleep."

" 'Kay. I'll try."

She stepped over to Dad and plucked the magazine from his hands, tossing it onto David's desk.

"Hey!" Dad exclaimed. "Gimme that!"

"Your bedtime, too, fella," she said as she left the room.

"You can read it later, Dad," David whispered. "It's a good one."

Dad moved to David's side and sat on the edge of the bed. "Okay."

"Hey, your base commander came to our school today."

"Mad Dog Wilson?" he said and laughed. "Same old thing, huh?"

"Yeah. Public relations for the base, I guess."

"You guess, huh?"

"We talked about the new radar a little. I got to explain how it works."

"Good for you. Just stick with me, kid. I'll show you the ropes."

Distant thunder rolled ominously through the sky and David's eyes grew. "Did you hear that?"

"Hear what?"

"Thunder. Jeez, Dad, you must be getting pretty old. You're losing your hearing already."

Dad kissed him and said, "Goodnight, wise guy." He stood and went to the door.

David leaned over the foot of the bed and turned on the small planetarium that was on his toy box. When Dad flicked the light off, the room became a window to outer space. The ceiling and walls were suddenly covered with pinpoints of light arranged to form a vast night sky all in one room.

Dad started to close the door, stopped, and stepped back inside. "Almost forgot," he said, reaching into his pocket. He held up a shiny new penny in a plastic case. "Here, a fifty-eight-D in mint condition."

David sat up in bed. "Wow!" Spots of light sparked off the shiny penny. "Thanks, Dad!"

"Sure." He looked around the starry room a moment until he spotted David's shirt hanging on the back of a chair by the desk. "I'll leave it for you here in your shirt pocket." He dropped the penny in the pocket and went back to the door.

"Thanks," David said. "I love you, Dad."

"Love you, too, Champ. Good night."

He slowly pulled the door closed until all the light from the hall was blocked from the room, leaving David to gaze at the stars and constellations around him. After a moment, he swept the covers back and got out of bed, then went to the window where his telescope waited, staring blankly out at the night.

He slid the window up and looked through the telescope, trying to find the meteors, hoping he'd be able to follow their rapid course. They moved too fast for his telescope, though, so he stepped around it and sat on the windowsill.

Although none were as bright as the one he and Dad had witnessed earlier, he could still see them, flitting through the sky like distant thoughts being rejected by God. The thought made him smile.

David hoped to be out there one day, to see firsthand what there was to see, to perhaps be the first astronaut ever to make contact with another intelligence . . . whatever kind of intelligence there was in space. He stared through his window at the endless sky, which came to life now and then with more meteorites, and imagined himself in a sleek spacesuit, at the controls of a ship, traveling swiftly and silently through space. . . .

A flicker of lightning brought him from his reverie. It was followed by the rumble of far-off thunder. A storm was coming in.

He pushed away from the sill and crossed the room, getting into bed, still clinging to his thoughts of the future, of space travel and discovery.

Turning on his side and snuggling into the pillow, David watched the stars on his walls and slowly, comfortably drifted off to sleep.

Chapter Four

David sat bolt upright in bed, suddenly jarred from his sleep by a shattering crash of thunder and the howl of wind raging around the corners of the house.

The planetarium was still shining stars onto his wall.

The alarm clock beside his bed read 4:40.

He had left the window open and rain was blowing into the room, bringing with it a biting chill.

David suddenly felt rather dizzy. He realized, looking around him, that the planetarium by his bed was slowly beginning to turn, sending the stars around and around the room. He rubbed his eyes, still puffy with sleep, and blinked them several times, puzzled. He hadn't flipped the rotate switch, and yet that was what it was doing. He sat up straighter in bed as the stars began to move faster and faster, creating a tornado of light around him. Soon they were no longer specks but silent streaks whizzing over the walls and ceiling.

A bright flash of lightning filled the room with white

and startled David; he pressed himself against the headboard and lifted a hand before his eyes. The lightning seemed to last a long time, much longer than usual.

"Jeeeeez," he breathed.

Catlike hissing and spitting sounds made David look over the foot of the bed. The planetarium was spinning madly, shooting sparks and puffing smoke in little clouds. The room was suddenly black and silent except for the sounds of the storm outside.

David kicked the covers aside and hurried to the window. He gripped the sash to pull it down when the rain stopped—not gradually, as rain usually does, but all at once, leaving behind it an eerie stillness.

Pushing the window all the way open again, David looked outside and listened. Only the sound of water dripping softly from the trees could be heard. The moon and stars were gone, hidden behind dark storm clouds. It was so dark, David could barely see anything outside; the hill was just a dim shape in the distance.

As he gazed out the window, David realized how tense he felt. Beneath his white pajamas, his limbs were rigid as sticks and there was a tightness in his chest that came only with . . . dread. Something was not right.

The silence outside was too heavy, too thick, worse, even, than the silence that followed Mrs. McKeltch's "*One*, two, *three*, four, *five!*"

David leaned toward the window, palms flat on the sill, and waited, although for what he did not know. The whole night seemed to be waiting . . . for something.

And then it came, a sound so sudden and loud that it

ripped the silence jaggedly in two—a horrible, throbbing sound so deep and massive that David could not only hear it, he could feel it in the very marrow of his bones, in the windowsill beneath his hands, vibrating the air around him. David was so terrified that, for a moment, he could not move a muscle. His hands felt like lead weights when he finally lifted them from the windowsill and reached over his head, grabbed the sash, and pulled it down.

It would not budge.

With a frightened groan, David tried again, putting all his weight into it, lifting his feet from the floor, hanging, for just an instant, from the sash.

The window was sturdy as stone.

He dropped his hands to his sides and turned away from the window, then started to hurry down the hall and wake his parents, when the room slowly began to fill with a soft light. Brighter and brighter . . .

David looked out the window again and his jaw hung loosely, his eyes became so wide that they felt like they might pop from their sockets.

There were lights cutting through the cloud layer, solid bars of light that landed on the ground in bright circles, flashing with a strobe effect, each appearing then disappearing in a heartbeat, beams of bluish-white dancing in a strange, hypnotic rhythm so precise, so perfect, that it seemed important, significant.

David gawked at the lights darting over the ground until something above caught his eye, something descending from the sky, easing through the thick clouds, something glowing and huge, so huge that its size alone filled David's stomach with an icy ache. Its light diffused outward through the storm clouds, giving them a shimmering glow. It was a sphere that seemed, at first, to be as big as a building. But as it continued to descend, more and more of it became visible and David realized that it was far bigger than any building he'd ever seen.

The sphere—metallic, glowing a bright bluish-silver—began to shift its shape. As if it were an enormous water balloon, it flattened itself into a disc, like a giant, glowing Frisbee. It wobbled slightly and changed again, first into a bottle shape, then, smoothly, it became more rectangular, like one of those jars Grandma Gardiner used to can peaches in every summer. It thinned out then, elongating itself into a spear shape, falling lower and lower until it disappeared behind the hill. It continued to glow, its light reflecting off the clouds overhead, and when David placed his hands on the sill again, he could still feel the vibration of that awful, gut-wrenching thrum.

Then they both faded, the light and the sound.

The night, once again, was silent.

An explosion of lightning was followed by thunder, more distant now. With a howl of wind, the rain began to fall again, as if it had never stopped.

Blinking his eyes with shock, David leaned forward, sticking his head out the window a bit, looking all around, his heart pounding like the footsteps of a giant in his chest.

Nothing. Only the yard, the hill, and the storm.

David pulled his head back just as the window slammed shut loudly. He jumped back with a startled cry, then stood like an ice statue, staring with wild-eyed fear and wonder at the night, waiting for something more to happen.

The rain fell with a vengeance.

Lightning brought an instant of distorted daylight.

Thunder purred sedately, more evenly than before.

The wind made the trees murmur among themselves.

Like a racehorse from the gate, David bolted from his room and ran down the hall, his feet thumping on the floor. Without knocking, he threw open the door of his parents' bedroom and hurried to their bedside, stopping so suddenly he nearly fell on his face.

"Dad! Mom!"

They were motionless lumps beneath the covers.

"Dad! Mom!" David cried again, grabbing the lump on his dad's side and shaking it urgently.

Dad jerked awake, turned over and tried to sit up, his eyes squinting. "Whuh-Da-David, what's wrong?"

David was screaming now, his whole body crawling with goose pimples. "You've gotta come! You've gotta come see, a, a UFO! A big one! It went down over the hill! I saw it!"

Wearily, Dad pulled the covers aside and swung his legs over the edge of the bed. Mom simply stirred beneath her blankets.

"C'mon," Dad said to her.

She rolled over and groaned, "Ooohhh, I'm *so* glad you got him a telescope."

David ran back down the hall to his bedroom and stopped in his doorway. He turned to see his dad staggering slowly from the far bedroom, tying the belt of his robe. David ran back and grabbed Dad's arm. "C'mon, c'mon, Dad!"

"Okay, Champ, okay." He allowed David to lead him, stumbling, to the bedroom, then to the window. Mom was not far behind.

Dad gripped the sash, opened the window, and all

three of them leaned forward to look outside. Mom yawned loudly, halfheartedly covering her mouth.

The rain was falling lightly now and water babbled as it fell from the rain gutter above the window. A flicker of sheet lightning illuminated the peaceful hill; the scrub pines were nodding in the gentle wind.

David couldn't believe it. Not only was there nothing out of the ordinary in sight, but even the storm had calmed.

"But . . . it was *there!*" David shouted, pointing toward the hill. "It was huge! And it glowed really bright with this strange light! And it went down over there, right behind the hill!" He stepped back as his mom and dad turned to him. His mom yawned again; Dad leaned against the windowsill.

Fear suddenly caused a gurgle in David's stomach. He wished that he hadn't run to them because he could almost hear the thoughts in their heads. They would think he'd been dreaming, having another of those nightmares. When they went back to bed, after David had left the room, Mom might say something like, "Think we should send David back to Dr. Wycliffe?"

And Dad might say, "Maybe so. He seemed pretty shook up."

He had to convince them, he *had* to make them believe it was real and not just a dream.

"I bet it was ball lightning," Dad said quietly.

"I know what ball lightning is, Dad! No, no, this was something else!" David sighed, suddenly feeling very tired and helpless. He looked out the window at the hill. "No, it was a UFO. It must have been."

Mom folded her arms before her, snuggling warmly into her robe, and turned to Dad. "Could it have been something from the base?" she asked.

"No, Mom," David said before Dad could reply. "It wasn't a plane. It wasn't from . . ." He paused, debating whether or not to speak the words on his lips. "It wasn't from Earth."

"Maybe it was a meteorite," Dad suggested.

"*No way,* Dad! It was too big, too bright. It was even brighter than the big one we saw! And louder! It was so loud, it shook the house! I can't *believe* you didn't wake up!"

Mom and Dad stared at David blankly, then looked out the window again.

Remembering the planetarium, David grabbed his dad's hand. "C'mere, Dad! Look what it did!" He led him to the foot of his bed and pointed to the lifeless machine, now spotted with black. "See? It freaked out my planetarium, made it throw sparks and everything! It just blew up!"

Dad touched it with his toe. Suddenly, his face changed. His left eyebrow moved down over his eye and the other one popped up. He was concerned and, more importantly, *interested!*

"Tell you what, Champ," Dad said thoughtfully, slowly walking back to the window and looking out at the hill. "I'll take a look in the morning, when it's light."

"But, Dad, it could be—"

"It's cold and rainy and dark out there, David. I'll look in the morning before breakfast, I promise."

David looked down at his bare feet and clenched his teeth. Reluctantly, he said, "Okay."

Dad closed the window, then bent down and swept David off his feet, hefting him over his shoulder and carrying him to the bed. "*You,*" he growled, "go back to sleep!" He tossed him onto the bed, pulled the covers over him, and smiled. "In the morning. I promise." He kissed David on the forehead. "Good night again, Champ."

"Night, Dad."

They left the room, closing the door quietly. As they went down the hall, David could hear their muffled, hushed voices and was able to distinguish a few words.

". . . those nightmares again . . ." Dad said quietly.

". . . talk to Dr. Wycliffe?" Mom asked.

After a few moments, their bedroom door closed softly.

David curled up under the covers and clenched his eyes shut, his whole body tense. He was angry at himself for waking them. He realized he should never have told them what he'd seen; now they were talking about sending him to Dr. Wycliffe again, just as he'd thought they would. Well, he wouldn't go.

"I *won't!*" he mumbled into his pillow.

David wrapped an arm around his pillow and held it close to him, wishing he'd just gone outside himself to see what had gone down in the sand pit instead of waking Mom and Dad. When he found out what it was, he could've come back to the house and gotten them, taken them to it, *proved* to them that he'd really seen something.

I can still do that! he thought as he rolled out of bed and slid his feet into his slippers. He grabbed his robe from the bedpost, then went to his night stand and opened the top drawer. He took out his flashlight and flicked it on; it worked. Before leaving the room, David peeked over the edge of Jasper's terrarium. The lizard's head was poking out from under a piece of bark.

"I'll be right back," David whispered.

He put the flashlight in the pocket of his plaid robe and quietly left the room, crept down the hall, and ran his hand along the bannister as he silently tiptoed down the stairs.

Once through the kitchen, he found the back door unlocked. That was odd; Dad was usually very careful about locking all the doors at night. Maybe after the excitement of the meteor shower, it had slipped his mind. David pushed the screen door open gradually, just a bit at a time, so the loud screech wouldn't wake Mom and Dad.

Outside, the rain had stopped and stars were beginning to twinkle through breaks in the clouds. A low mist hovered ghostlike over the ground.

David took the flashlight from his pocket as he crossed the wet grass and flicked it on when he reached the trail. In the mist, the beam of light became solid, almost tangible, and David swept it cautiously back and forth before him as a blind man would his cane.

The trail was smooth, undisturbed. There was no sign of what David had seen earlier.

The night was alive with sounds.

Frogs croaked in the darkness.

Crickets chirped with a cheerfulness that seemed sinister in the night.

An owl hooted and shifted in the branches overhead.

Tentacles of mist curled around the posts of the split-rail fence; they seemed to be trying to escape the beam of David's flashlight.

He spotted something on the ground and squatted down, shining the light before him. Footprints in the rain-softened ground were headed over the hill. He followed them with his eyes until they disappeared over the top.

Before David could stand again, something slapped onto his shoulder and, with a scream of fright, David fell on his side and rolled back down the trail, dropping the flashlight and swiping at the thing on his shoulder. The flashlight rolled down the path with him, its light darting over the ground and the bushes around David, adding to his panic.

David got on his hands and knees, gasping, and looked around frantically. A few feet away, staring at him stupidly, was a frog, fat and moist. Its throat bulged as it croaked.

David felt the fear washing off him as he touched his shoulder; it was wet and sticky.

"Stupid frog," he whispered. He got up, brushing himself off, then picked up the frog. It squirmed in his hand restlessly. David tossed it to the side of the path, then realized that Copper Hill was thick with frogs. They seemed to come out in force at that moment, hopping this way and that over the path, croaking loudly, filling the night with their deep, throaty sounds.

David stepped over to his flashlight, which was no longer shining. He picked it up and flicked it a few times. It wouldn't work. As he slipped it into his pocket again, wondering what to do next, he heard a soft *crunch:* leaves underfoot.

A twig snapped.

More leaves whispered.

Footsteps.

Slowly, with a tightness building in his chest, he turned and looked up the hill.

The sky above the hill was beginning to glow with the light of dawn and against the dim haze, a figure rose over the hill's crest, walking slowly toward David.

"Dad?" David asked timidly. Then, when he was certain, he took a couple steps up the path. "Dad!"

He continued walking over the hill, but said nothing. His bathrobe hung on him sloppily, the untied belt dangling at his sides. He seemed tired, maybe even a little sick. David noticed, as he got closer, that Dad had that look on his face that often remained a day or so after the New Year's Eve party at the base: tense, squeamish.

"Did you see anything, Dad?" David asked.

He didn't even seem to notice David.

"Dad? Are you all right?"

Dad's face relaxed, just a little, and he looked down at David, almost, but not quite, smiling. "Sure. Fine." But he didn't stop walking. David's presence was apparently forgotten once again and the tight, sickly expression returned to Dad's face as he walked by David.

Turning slowly as Dad passed, watching him head toward the house, David saw him stumble, then regain his balance. He looked down at Dad's feet. On one foot he wore a dirty, ragged slipper; the other was muddy and bare. He rolled his head around as he walked, rubbing his neck as if it ached.

David frowned as Dad crossed the back yard and went into the house. Something was not right. Why was he wearing only one slipper? And why did he have that nauseated look on his face? He hadn't even told David to go back to bed!

Something was definitely not right.

Stepping over frogs, David made his way slowly to the house, hoping Dad would be in bed when he got there. He didn't like to see him like that. Maybe he would be better in the morning.

Looking at the sky, which was glowing a little brighter, David thought, *It is morning.*

In his room, David sat on the edge of the bed, nibbling on his lower lip and nervously twitching a foot.

Coming up the stairs, he'd heard movement down the hall in his parents' room. He'd ducked into his bedroom and shut the door, then, after a moment of thought, he'd locked it.

The hall was silent for a while, then David heard his dad's hushed voice and more movement. The hall light was flicked on and its glow seeped under David's bedroom door.

Soft footsteps.

The familiar creak of the floor just above the stairs.

The footsteps stopped for a moment, then continued along the hall toward David's room. He pushed himself back on the bed, hugged his knees to his chest, and pressed against the headboard.

The light beneath the door was darkened by two feet.

"David?" Dad asked softly.

David grabbed his covers and pulled them over him, curling up in his robe.

"You asleep?"

Turning his back to his dad's voice, David closed his eyes tightly, feeling cold.

The doorknob turned several times, its metallic clicks sounding like explosions in David's ears.

His heart was beating so hard that he was afraid Dad might hear. He remained still, waiting, until he heard his dad's footsteps receding down the hall. David opened his eyes, but he didn't move. He decided he wouldn't go downstairs until he knew Mom was up.

Guilt nibbled at David's insides. He was angry at himself for feeling the way he did toward his dad. He loved Dad, trusted him, and knew that Dad would never do anything to hurt him.

But something was wrong. Something was different.

David got out of bed and quietly walked to the window. In the growing light of dawn, Copper Hill was a maze of shadows. Beyond and out of sight lay the sand pit.

What did Dad find over there? David wondered. His next thought brought with it a deep chill: *What found him?*

Chapter Five

David stood at his bedroom door—showered, dressed, and ready for school. He had his books in his backpack, his pennies in his pouch. He faced the closed door for several moments before steeling himself, opening it, and stepping into the hall.

His parents' bedroom door was closed. There was no one in sight. David could smell something cooking in the kitchen. He hoped that Mom was up.

On his way down the stairs, he heard his mom muttering in the kitchen.

"On the journal side," she said, "we have our receipts . . . a little sales . . . some invoices. . . ."

David stopped at the foot of the stairs. He couldn't tell if she was talking to Dad or just to herself.

"Okay, in our ledger, we have accounts receivable . . . and payments . . . sundries. . . ."

David went to the kitchen door and looked around.

Dad was nowhere in sight. Mom was at the small bar that came off the counter, hunched over her books. He cleared his throat and asked, "Where's Dad?"

"Did you make your bed?" she asked without looking up.

"It's made." He went into the kitchen and peered over her shoulder. He was so surprised at what he saw that he blinked several times, unable to suppress a tickled grin. She was writing notes on her fingers! Mom was *cheating!* "Mom, what . . . what are you doing?"

With a startled gasp, she spun away from the bar. "Nothing!" She slapped her books closed and pressed her hands on the covers. "Nothing," she said again. "It's . . . not what you think."

"You'll get caught," he said, still grinning.

Her face relaxed and she smirked. "Nah," she whispered, "not me."

David could tell she was embarrassed at being caught and decided to change the subject. "Mom, where's—"

"George," she interrupted, looking over David's shoulder, "you're not dressed?"

David spun around and almost pushed his face into Dad's stomach. He was still in his bathrobe, standing so close that David had to tilt his head way back to see his face. Dad looked down at David.

No smile.

No good morning.

No expression at all except that vague, queasy look.

David took a timid step back.

Dad had not yet combed his hair and spikes of it stuck out on the sides. His jaw was darkened by a shadow of stubble. One hand was in the pocket of his bathrobe, which looked mussed and slept in. His left foot was still bare and dirty.

"What happened to your other slipper, Dad?" David asked reluctantly.

"I lost it."

"Do you want coffee?" Mom asked.

Dad seemed uncertain. "Ummm . . . yeah."

Mom poured some and handed him the steaming cup. Dad set it on the table.

"George," Mom said, tilting her head as she looked him over, "is anything wrong with you? Are you all right, hon?"

Half of Dad's mouth curled into a boyish smile as he shrugged. "It's kind of muddy out there."

"Are you sure there wasn't anything over the hill, Dad?" David asked.

Dad looked down at him. His face was a blank stare for what seemed a long time, then he smiled fully, slowly extending his hand and touching his forefinger to David's nose.

"Nothing," he said. "It was just . . . a bad . . . dream. That's all." He pulled a chair out and seated himself at the table.

"Waffles are coming up," Mom said cheerily, tending to breakfast.

David hardly heard her. He leaned against the bar silently watching Dad.

Tendrils of steam curled under Dad's nose as he lifted the cup of coffee to his mouth. Touching the rim to his lips, he began to gulp the coffee, taking big, long swallows until it was gone.

David put a hand on the edge of the bar and clutched

until his knuckles were white as he watched steam flow from his dad's mouth. He expected a pained reaction, at least a wince. The coffee had obviously been very hot and drinking it so fast *must* have hurt! Dad only smacked his lips a few times and stood, taking the empty cup back to the pot for a refill.

Amazed, David followed him with his eyes and noticed something on the back of his neck, something small and dark. He only got a glimpse of it before Dad turned from the coffeepot.

"I could've gotten that, hon," Mom said, dishing up breakfast.

Dad ignored her, took the small bottle of saccharine tablets from the counter, and returned to the table. As he scooted his chair up, David stepped behind him and looked at his neck.

It was a cut, puffy and bruised, with black dried blood still clinging to it, just above the collar of Dad's bathrobe.

"What happened to your neck, Dad?" David asked, alarmed.

Dad immediately put a hand over the spot, fingering it.

"A branch must've nicked me," he said casually, adjusting his collar.

David stepped closer, trying to get another look at the cut, but it was covered by the collar.

Dad turned and smiled at him. "Sit down, David. Breakfast is ready."

As David took his seat, Dad poured saccharine tablets into his coffee. He plopped nearly half the little white tablets into his cup.

Mom turned from the counter with a plate in each

hand, setting them on the table. "Honey," she said to Dad, "why don't you let me take a look at it?"

"It's nothing."

"Let me see. It might need a Band-Aid. I could—"

"*No!*" Dad snapped.

Mom flinched at his tone. "Okay. Fine." She turned to David. "Eat your breakfast before it gets cold. I've got to go."

David ignored his mother as she bent down and kissed him on the head, staring instead at Dad, who poured the rest of the saccharine tablets into his coffee, emptying the bottle. He took a few big gulps of the coffee, looking satisfied as more steam swirled from his lips.

"Bye, darling," Mom said, kissing Dad, too. Then she gathered her books from the counter and started out of the kitchen.

"Mom!" David said, his back stiff. He wanted desperately for her to stay. Something was wrong.

"Hurry up and eat, David, or you'll be late again," she called over her shoulder as she disappeared through the doorway.

David stared at the empty doorway until he heard the front door close. He looked at the clock: 7:20. The ticking seemed thunderous in the silence.

Dad stared across the table at David, his breakfast ignored, steam rising from his cup.

Mom knocked on the kitchen window, startling David. "You're not eating!" she exclaimed through the glass. She turned and hurried to the car.

David bit his lip, fighting the urge to bound out of the kitchen and stop her. What would he say? If he tried to explain to her the icy dread that was growing inside him, he would only sound crazy. With a helpless, sinking feeling, he watched her back the car out of the driveway and disappear down the road.

David looked at his breakfast. His stomach was burning with tension and the mere thought of putting the waffles and eggs and orange wedges into his mouth made his throat feel tight.

Dad continued to stare unflinchingly at David. His face was stone, his eyes empty and unblinking.

He's just not feeling well, David thought, trying to reassure himself. *He's probably coming down the with flu, that's all.* But it didn't work. Dad's stare did not waver and David began to feel as if he were being held in a giant steel fist that was slowly clenching tighter and tighter.

David tried to speak, but his throat was dry and only croaked. He coughed, then said, "I . . . I don't think I'm very hungry."

No reaction. Neither a twitch of his cheek nor a blink of his eyes. Then Dad pushed his chair from the table and stood, never taking his eyes from David. He walked around the table until he was standing beside David, tall and straight. He took David's arm.

David suddenly felt as if the wind had been knocked from his lungs. He wanted to jerk his arm away, to scream, *Get away from me! Don't touch me!* He wanted to run from the house as fast as he could and not come back until Mom was home. But how could he do such a thing to his own dad?

Quietly, his voice cutting through the silence like a new razor blade, Dad said, "Let me walk you to the bus stop."

Slowly, David stood. His knees felt rubbery and the bag hanging from his shoulder suddenly felt like a cement block. Dad's grip on his elbow was not tight, but neither was it gentle. David's feet were made of lead and it was only with effort that he left the kitchen at his dad's side.

They crossed the living room and went out the front door. It wasn't until they were starting down the driveway that David mustered the nerve to look up at his dad.

He was still staring at David, even as he walked, as if he'd never looked away. His lips were smiling but his eyes were not. When they reached the end of the driveway, Dad finally let go of David's arm.

Slipping his hands into the pockets of his bathrobe, Dad turned and gazed toward Copper Hill.

"You know, you were right, son," Dad said. He looked down at David. "There *is* something over the hill."

David tensed. "What?"

Dad smiled again, but still his eyes remained cold. "Come on. I'll show you."

David suddenly did not want to see whatever lay beyond Copper Hill. "No, Dad," he said quietly, shrinking back a step.

Still smiling, Dad reached for his hand.

"Dad . . ."

His smile did not waver as he grabbed David's hand and began pulling him hard toward the house.

"No!" David shouted, trying to jerk his hand away. "What are you doing?" He wrenched his hand from his dad's grip. David could hear the distant rumble of the bus rounding the corner down the road.

Dad's cold smile dissolved into a mocking sneer. "What's the matter, son," he said, "*afraid* of something?"

David took a broad step back, staring up in disbelief

at his dad. The tiny smile wrinkles on his face no longer seemed warm and friendly, and his eyes were like a stranger's, unfamiliar and uncaring.

The bus slowed as it neared, and finally stopped in front of the driveway. The sound of the doors clattering open brought a rush of relief David never thought he'd feel at the arrival of his school bus. Hitching his backpack up with a shrug, David backed toward the bus.

The man standing in the driveway was not his dad. He looked like him; he wore his clothes. But David knew that George Gardiner was not behind those eyes.

As David put one foot on the bus step, Dad grinned, lifted a hand slowly, and waved.

"See you this afternoon," he said. Then he added, in a tone that was somehow not right, that had behind it the sound of glass being cut, "Champ."

David stepped up into the bus and the doors closed. He could not have felt more threatened had there been a gun at his head.

Chapter Six

When David got to class that morning, there were dead frogs split open like pomegranates on the desks. Other frogs, very much alive, threw themselves against the glass sides of the jars in which they were trapped on Mrs. McKeltch's desk, as if they sensed their fate.

David plopped down at his desk, frowning. His stomach was upset and one foot kicked the desk leg nervously. He could not erase the image of his dad standing in the driveway, looking a mess, waving his hand and smiling falsely as David boarded the bus. The way he felt, he dreaded sitting through classes that day. But he also dreaded going home.

Mrs. McKeltch divided the students into pairs as they came in and assigned each pair to a dissected frog.

David's partner was Heather. She sat beside him,

her brown hair in a ponytail, and stared with a curled lip at the frog.

"That's disgusting," she whispered.

Although he did not feel like talking, David said, "It's just a frog."

"But all its . . . its *insides* are showing."

"You have them, too, you know."

She turned to him and wrinkled her nose. "Don't say that. I don't *want* to know."

When the last bell rang, Mrs. McKeltch stood before her desk holding a stack of papers to her bosom. Her face was stern and her gray hair was arranged in its usual tight curls and sharp little waves. The friendly morning chatter among the students was silenced by her stare.

"These papers," Mrs. McKeltch said, "are consent forms for the upcoming field trip. Your parents *must* sign them or you will not be allowed to go and you will get an F for the day." She began walking up and down the aisles between the desks, passing the papers to her students. "So, have your parents sign them tonight and bring them back to me promptly in the morning."

When she came to David and held out the paper, she gave him a glare that seemed to warn: *Behave today, or else*.

When she was finished, Mrs. McKeltch returned to her desk and gestured to the frogs hopping around in their jars. "I collected these fresh specimens yesterday from the marsh area adjacent to Copper Hill. When we're finished here this morning, *these* frogs—" She pointed to those on her desk, then to the dissected frogs before the students. "—will look like the frogs you have before you." She lifted a shoe box from her desk and took from it a small object with a shiny blade.

"This is a scalpel. It is very sharp so be extremely careful when using it." As she passed out the scalpels, she said, "Before we start the dissection, we're going to review what we've learned about frogs in the past week." She went to the front of the classroom and pulled down a chart over the blackboard. She pointed to the colorful diagram of a dissected frog and asked, "Who can tell me what these two red sacs are?"

The class was silent.

"You may refer to the frogs in front of you if it will help," Mrs. McKeltch said, frustrated.

Marcy Young raised her hand, her eyes fixed on the dissected frog.

"Yes, Marcy?" Mrs. McKeltch said, smiling her iguana smile.

Still looking down at her frog, Marcy asked, "Which ones, Mrs. McKeltch?"

When Mrs. McKeltch went to the back of the class to help Marcy, a frog flew through the air behind her and slapped onto Heather's chest, sliding into her lap, unseen by the teacher.

"*Gawd!*" Heather squealed, startling David.

He turned to see Kevin (*Who else?* he thought) laughing into his palm across the room. Not at all in the mood for Kevin, David grabbed the frog from Heather's lap and half stood, putting his hand on the desktop. He threw the frog at Kevin just as Mrs. McKeltch turned around.

"David Gardiner!" she snapped.

He paid little attention to her because he'd put his hand right on the scalpel; a small cut on the outer edge of his palm had begun to bleed.

"That may be the way you behave at home," Mrs.

McKeltch went on, "but it's not the way you'll behave in *my* classroom!" The students began laughing at David until Mrs. McKeltch raised her hand and said, "*One*, two, *three*, four, *five!*"

Instant silence.

"Oh God, he's bleeding!" Heather gasped, gawking with wide eyes at David's hand.

Mrs. McKeltch approached David's desk and towered over him like a building. Her fists were clenched at her sides and her lips were pressed so tightly together they'd become pale.

"Heather," she said, her eyes boring into David, "you supervise them while I take this uncontrolled young man to the school nurse."

"Yes, ma'am," Heather said softly. She gave David a look of silent apology.

Mrs. McKeltch grabbed David's wrist and dragged him out of the room, stopping in the hall to examine his cut briefly. Her eyes narrowed to slits and a cold smile pulled at her lips as she led him down the hall holding his wrist in an iron grip. "I hope you need a tetanus shot," she hissed.

"That's good news, Mrs. Beacham," Linda said into the phone, sitting on the edge of her desk. "I'm glad it wasn't a break."

She could hear someone stopping outside her office door and tried to wrap up the conversation.

"Just keep her off the foot for a few days and tell her—"

The door opened and Mrs. McKeltch stormed in, her face tight, holding the hand of the boy who Linda had run into the day before.

"Ms. Magnuson," Mrs. McKeltch said angrily, "David here has gone ahead and cut himself. It probably serves him right."

Linda held up a palm, trying to listen to Mrs. Beacham. "Okay, that's fine," she said. "Tell her that we'll miss her here at school. All right, thank you." She hung up the phone and turned in time to see Mrs. McKeltch rolling her eyes, annoyed at having to wait. "I'm sorry," Linda said with a smile. "What's wrong?"

"I *said* this silly boy has cut himself! I don't know what he's gotten into. He's . . . he's simply uncontrollable."

Children behave only as well as they're treated, Linda thought, wanting to say it aloud, but knowing better. She put a hand on David's shoulder and squeezed reassuringly. "I'll take it from here, Mrs. McKletch," she said, realizing her mistake the moment it was out of her mouth.

"It's Mc*Keltch,*" the teacher snapped, her nostrils flaring. She turned and stalked out, slamming the office door so hard it rattled the pictures on the walls.

Linda sighed with relief and smiled down at David. He was holding his injured hand gingerly with the other, frowning deeply.

"Why don't you come back here and sit down," she said, trying to sound as pleasant as possible to make up for Mrs. McKeltch's harsh behavior. The woman made her angry, but she held it in, deciding the boy had seen enough anger for one day.

She led him into the examination room and helped him up onto the cushioned table, taking his hand carefully in hers. The cut was bleeding quite a bit, but it wasn't bad.

"I think you'll live," she said.

He looked away, his eyes fixed blankly on a stack of paper towels on the counter by the sink. There were more frown lines on his forehead than seemed fitting for a boy so young.

"Hey," Linda said, patting his arm, "don't worry about her, okay? Mrs. McKeltch, I mean. She's just . . . like that." She smiled, but got no reaction. "Okay?"

He looked at her and nodded, chewing his lip.

Linda got her tray of supplies and placed it next to David. "You sure get around this place, don't you?"

"Yeah. I guess."

Dipping a swab into a bottle of iodine, she said, "Now, this stuff stings a little, so watch out, okay?" She gently tended the cut, cautiously watching David's face for a reaction. But he did not even flinch. In fact, he didn't even seem to notice the stinging medicine; he was staring blankly again, this time at a picture on the wall across from him. He seemed preoccupied, perhaps even troubled, as if the cut on his hand were the least of his worries.

"Tough guy, huh?" Linda asked.

David shrugged, watching as she put a Band-Aid over the cut. He looked at her thoughtfully for a moment, then said, "So you're the new nurse, huh?"

"Oh, that's right, I never introduced myself. I'm Linda Magnuson." She took David's hand in hers and shook it, realizing, as David squirmed in pain and jerked his hand back, holding it to his stomach protectively, that she shook the wrong hand. "David!" Linda gasped, covering her mouth. "I'm sorry, David, really! I'm so sorry." She touched his arm and leaned forward anxiously, hoping she hadn't hurt him badly. "Are you okay?"

A smile slowly grew on David's face; he seemed touched by her concern. "Yeah, don't worry about it. It's okay."

Brushing aside a few strands of her blond hair, she stepped back. "Good. Well," she joined her hands before her, "you should probably get back to class."

David scooted off the edge of the table and started out of the room, still holding his hand.

Linda realized that he was moving very slowly. And he was frowning again, head bowed, eyes distant.

"Hey," Linda said.

David turned, looked up at her, and blinked a few times. "Hm?"

"Is anything wrong, David? Anything bothering you? If there is, I want you to know you can talk to me about it. I'm a good listener."

He thought about that a moment, seemed to consider saying something, his lips slightly pursed, his head cocked to one side. Then he shook his head and said, "No. Nothing."

"Okay." She reached down and brushed his bangs from his forehead. "You be careful with that hand now, okay?"

"I will." He turned and left the office, closing the door softly.

Linda gritted her teeth, her anger at Mrs. McKeltch coming back with force. How could she treat children so coldly? Didn't she think they were human? Didn't she think they had feelings just like everybody else? *Well,* Linda thought, *everybody, that is, except Mrs.*

McKeltch. She returned to her desk to make some phone calls.

Going home on the bus, David was the only passenger who remained totally silent. He peered out the window, wondering what he would find at home, wondering if Dad would still be there, if he would be better or . . . what if Mom started acting strange like Dad? David immediately rejected the thought, wanting to deal with only one problem at a time.

"What the heck's your problem?" Doug asked.

"Huh?"

"What's your problem? You mad or something?"

"Oh, no." David shook his head.

"Then how come you're being so quiet? Are you sick?"

"No. But I think my dad might be. I'm worried about him."

"How come?"

"Well, he . . . I don't know, he just kinda got weird this morning."

"Oh, jeez, don't worry about that."

David turned to him for an explanation.

"My dad does that all the time. So does Mom. All parents do. Parents are weird," he said with a wave of his hand. "They go through these moods, you know? My mom tells me I'll understand when I grow up. But I don't think I *want* to understand the way they act sometimes. Nah, don't worry about it. It's nothin'."

"You think so?"

"Sure." Doug poked him in the ribs with his elbow. "Cheer up."

David smiled, feeling a little better. But his smile disappeared as soon his house came into view.

Dad's pickup truck was in the driveway.

Mom's car was nowhere in sight, but David realized it could be in the garage. David walked to the front of the bus and held onto a rail as it stopped. The doors opened. David couldn't move his feet from the top step. He held the cold rail and stared at his house. It was usually a welcome sight with its cheery windows and well-kept yard. Now it seemed threatening. The windows were like eyes that watched his every move and the front door, which was open wide, was a mouth patiently waiting for David to step inside.

"David . . ."

He turned to Mr. Bob. The driver waved a meaty hand at the door, motioning for him to get off.

"See ya tomorrow," Mr. Bob said.

David nodded. Before stepping down, he glanced toward the back of the bus at Doug. He was laughing with someone; David was forgotten. As the doors closed behind him and the bus rumbled away, David felt very alone. He watched the bus disappear down the road, then turned toward the house.

As he walked up the driveway, David looked around the yard for some sign of his parents, but saw nothing.

A soft breeze made hushed sounds in the trees.

Somewhere a bird sang.

As David neared the open door, he heard a strange hissing sound coming from inside the house. Frowning, he climbed the front steps and peeked inside. The living room was empty; the television was on.

"Dad?" David asked, taking a step inside.

No reply, no sound except for the hissing crackle of static from the television.

As David walked into the living room, the front door slammed explosively behind him and he jumped as if kicked. When he spun around, there was no one there.

The breeze? It wasn't strong enough.

"Dad?" he asked again, his voice cracking. He looked around again but the only eyes he met were the red bulbs of his toy robot standing against the wall, still and lifeless.

He turned to the television and reached for the button to turn it off, but the snowy fuzz that filled the screen suddenly disappeared and was replaced with a clear, colorful picture. On the screen, screaming crowds ran frantically through city streets as deadly beams shot back and forth over their heads. Buildings exploded, cars crashed. David frowned at the movie; he couldn't remember if he'd seen it or not. He folded his arms before him, allowing himself to become engrossed in the destruction, forgetting, for a moment, his anxiety.

Something began to whir mechanically behind him and a flat, emotionless voice said, "David Gardiner!"

David whirled around to see the foot-and-a-half-tall robot rolling toward him, arms waving, red eyes flashing, and a scream escaped him before he could stop it. He stepped back toward the television just before he saw Mom peek around the corner, grinning, the robot's remote control in her hand. The robot stopped.

"Mom!" David snapped, his heart pounding. "Don't do that!"

"Ha-ha, gotcha," she laughed, crossing the room and giving him a hug.

"Where's Dad?" he asked.

"I don't know. He's probably around here somewhere."

"No, he's not. I looked around."

Mom plopped onto the sofa and faced the television. "Oh, he probably got a ride to the base with one of the guys."

"No . . ." David fidgeted, the movie forgotten.

"Hey," Mom said, patting the sofa cushion beside her. "What's the matter?"

David sat beside her, trying to choose his words carefully. "Well, I'm not sure, Mom. Dad's . . . weirded out."

She put an arm around him and held him close. "Oh, you know your father, David. He's probably got a lot on his mind. He's a little worried about that bio-lab arm, you know. C'mon, don't worry. Okay?"

David looked away from her, unable to reply. He was worried. He was scared. And he felt as if he might never stop being scared again.

"What's this on the tube?"

David shrugged.

"*What?* There's a monster movie on TV and you don't know what it is?"

He shrugged again.

"You want something to eat, Champ?"

"No."

"Tell you what. I'll get some Oreos and milk and we can watch this movie together while we wait for your dad. How about that?"

David looked up and saw the anticipation in her face. He knew if he turned down Oreos and milk, not to mention a monster movie, she would worry. He decided to make her feel better.

"Okay," he said.

"Great." She hurried into the kitchen, saying over

her shoulder, "Don't worry, he'll be back soon. You'll see."

When George had not returned by the time dinner was ready, Ellen became concerned. Trying to remain calm for David, she put dinner in the oven to keep warm and called a few of George's friends from the base, casually asking them if they'd seen him.

"He wasn't at work today," Larry Hoban said. "Is anything wrong?"

"Oh, no," Ellen assured him, trying to keep the tremble out of her voice, "no, there's nothing wrong. I just needed him to do a favor for me, that's all. I wondered where he was. Thank you." She slammed the receiver in its cradle unintentionally hard.

He didn't even go to work! she thought, feeling the beginnings of panic set in.

"Okay," she said quietly to herself, picking up the phone again, "*now* I'm worried."

"Who're you calling?"

She looked up to see David standing on the staircase, his face tense with worry.

"I'm calling the police, honey," she replied, expecting to see alarm in his eyes. Instead, his shoulders slumped with what seemed to be relief.

"Good," he whispered, coming down the stairs. He stood beside her as she punched in the number on the phone.

Ellen's finger hesitated over the telephone's square buttons. It wasn't a number she dialed often—only once before, in fact. George had gone away on business for the weekend—some meeting in Washington, or something—and someone had tried to break into the house late at night. David had woken her, his eyes wide and fearful. Remembering how scared she had been, her hand trembled over the phone, and it occurred to her that she was calling the police, that George was gone, that something was not right, and her throat began to burn. She looked down at her son; he was waiting pensively, glancing from the phone to her and back again.

"David, honey," she said softly, "why don't you go out on the front porch? Maybe keep an eye out for your dad? Okay?"

He nodded slightly, turned and left.

"Jesus," she sighed, finishing the number.

Chief Ward said that he'd be there in just a few minutes. She hung up, stared at the phone a moment, then quickly crossed herself. She hadn't been a prac-ticing Catholic since high school, but she never hesi-tated to flick her hand up and down and back and forth when the waters got a little choppy.

She went out on the porch and sat down next to David.

"The chief said he'd be right over, Champ," she said, trying to sound cheery and unworried.

"You know, Mom," David said after a moment, "Dad has been acting kinda funny since this morning. Since he went over the hill."

"C'mon, David, I told you not to worry. He's just preoccupied, that's all." She watched him staring out at the driveway, twiddling his fingers together ner-vously. "David, are you sure *you're* feeling okay?"

"Yeah, Mom."

"Your nightmare bothering you?"

He turned to her suddenly, opened his mouth and took in a sharp breath to speak, his eyes wide, and she knew what he was going to say—*It wasn't a nightmare, Mom, really!*—but he closed his mouth, relaxed, and just shook his head. She put an arm around him and they sat in silence until the Willowbrook Police car drove up.

"Hi, Chief," Ellen said, standing to greet him as he got out of the car with a grunt, his round belly making his movements a bit awkward. Another man got out on the passenger side, younger, thinner. "Thanks for coming."

"No problem, Mrs. Gardiner," he said. "You know Officer Kenney?" He gestured to the younger man beside him.

"Ma'am," Kenney said with a nod, taking off his hat and revealing thick black hair.

"What seems to be the matter, Mrs. Gardiner?" the chief asked.

"Well, George isn't here. His pickup is, but he's not."

"Where do you think he might be?"

"I don't know," she shrugged. "I phoned a few of his friends, but they haven't seen him. David and I haven't spoken with him since this morning." She looked down at the boy to see his eyes suddenly widening, his face brightening with realization.

"Maybe he went back over the hill!" he said excitedly, grabbing Ellen's hand.

"David . . ." she said, hoping to quiet him. She didn't want him going on about UFOs with the police around.

The chief turned to David and bent down as much as his girth would allow. "What's that, David?"

"Copper Hill."

Ellen put a hand on his head. "George took a look

up there this morning. David thought he saw, um, an aircraft crash there last night."

"No, Mom!" David exclaimed, exasperated. "I saw a UFO! It had huge lights and everything! Just like in—"

"David, please, *stop* that." She smiled at the policemen, embarrassed. "Sorry."

The chief looked thoughtfully from David to Ellen. "Tell you what, Mrs. Gardiner," he said. "We'll go up there and have a look. Come on, Kenney."

They got their flashlights from the car, then Ellen and David followed them around the side of the house to the back yard. As they started toward the path, an ugly thought occurred to Ellen.

What if he's over there and something's wrong? What if he went back this morning, fell and hit his head, had no one to help him, and he's been lying there de—

She couldn't even *think* the word: dead.

"Let's wait here, David," Ellen said suddenly, holding David back, pulling him close to her.

Chief Ward and Officer Kenney headed up the hill, their flashlight beams bobbing before them. Ellen could hear their fading voices as they climbed.

"I haven't been up here since I was a kid," the chief puffed.

Kenney asked, "You hear anything about a plane crash?"

"Nah. The kid's just been watching too much TV."

Their flashlight beams swept back and forth before them as they went up the path. They stopped at the crest of the hill and gazed down at the sand pit. They seemed to be talking with one another, gesturing. Then they disappeared over the top.

Ellen felt her son put his arm around her waist and press himself close to her.

"Don't worry, honey," she said. "You know, maybe he went with someone to do some field work. That might be it. Don't worry, Dad's okay."

"I hope they are," he whispered with a nod toward the hill.

"Who?" she asked, looking down at him again. "You mean the chief? And Kenney?"

He said nothing.

Ellen squatted down beside him and turned him toward her. "David, exactly what do you think is over that hill?"

With another look toward the hill, slow and lingering, he said, "I don't know, Mom. But something is."

"Oh, David," she sighed, "I wish you wouldn't—"

Two quick footsteps made Ellen shriek as she shot to her feet and whirled around, coming face to face with George.

"My *God*, George," she snapped, instantly angry, pressing a hand to her chest. "You scared the *shit* out of me!"

Another man stepped out of the shadows behind him and stood at his side. Ellen had never seen him before. He was a tall man with a square jaw, a high forehead, and deep-set eyes.

George was wearing a suit, but it looked sloppy, as if he hadn't dressed with his usual care.

"This is Ed," he said. "Ed, this is my wife . . . my son."

Ed looked from David to Ellen, but said nothing.

Ellen's arm snaked around David's shoulders again, more protective than comforting this time. There was something about this man that made her very uncomfortable. In fact, there was something about George that didn't seem right. He looked and acted as if he were suffering from a heavy-duty hangover.

From beyond the hill, sounding hollow and mournful, a whippoorwill cried in the night, sending goose flesh across Ellen's back. She suddenly felt a chill in the warm, calm air.

"How do you do?" she said to Ed, breaking the frigid silence.

"Couldn't do much better," he replied. The words sounded as if they should be accompanied by a smile, but they weren't. In fact, Ed's face was quite blank. "And yourself?"

"I'm . . . yes, I'm fine." She turned to George and leaned her head forward, looking at him from beneath lowered brows. "George, where were you? David and I have been worried sick! I even called the police. They're over the hill looking for you now."

"Over the hill?" George asked quietly, looking beyond them toward Copper Hill.

"Well, I guess I better be going," Ed said. "I have to pick up Alice and Heather."

George turned to him, no smile, no handshake. Just a nod. "See you later, Ed."

The man turned and walked into the darkness, silent as a shadow.

"What *happened* to you?" Ellen asked George, even angrier than before. "And where did that guy come from? Who *is* he?"

"That's Heather's dad," David said, his voice quavering a bit. "She sits next to me in class. I think he's kinda . . . kinda weird, Dad."

George ignored him and turned to Ellen. "Ed works

for the phone company," he said. "The switching division." As if that explained everything.

"Since when are you working with the phone company?" she asked.

"We had a special meeting . . . the new hookup at the base."

Something about that reply didn't sound right. Ellen squinted at him curiously, but said nothing.

"Well," George said, holding his arms a few inches from his sides, then letting them drop, smiling faintly, "I'm home now."

David would have given anything to pull down the collar of Ed's coat to see if there was a cut on his neck. He had little doubt that he would find one. He had that odd, sickly look about him. . . .

Spots of light darted around David and his parents as the two policemen came back down the hill, flashlights in hand. David turned at the sound of their footsteps just in time to see Officer Kenney buttoning his collar clumsily with one hand and Chief Ward straightening his tie.

They're hiding their necks! David thought, wanting to scream, to run. He tugged on his mom's arm, whispering breathlessly, "Mom. *Mom!*"

She rested a hand on his head, but otherwise ignored him as the men approached.

"I see you're back," the chief said to Dad.

Dad nodded at them, just as he'd nodded to Ed, and they returned the gesture, as if they'd expected to see him!

Officer Kenney adjusted his hat, locking his eyes with David's. "Your little lad's got quite an imagination," he said rather sternly.

"Yes," Dad agreed, looking down at David. "I know."

The look in his eyes made David want to shrivel up and blow away. He suddenly felt hot and stuffy under the scrutiny of his dad and the policemen, and he wondered what kind of thoughts were slithering behind their cold, predatory eyes. Couldn't Mom see it? Was she blind to their behavior? Couldn't she tell they were watching him like a hawk would watch a field mouse?

"Thanks for coming, Chief," Mom said politely. "It looks like we found him ourselves."

"Everything's fine now," Dad told them. "You can go."

"Our pleasure," Chief Ward said.

Officer Kenney turned to Mom and tilted his head. "Bye, ma'am."

As they turned to leave, David thought he saw it, only for an instant, and not very clearly in the dark: a spot on the back of the chief's neck, darkened and puffy. Before he could be sure, Dad was leading him by the hand back to the house with Mom at his side. David craned his head around to get another look.

Officer Kenney was gingerly touching his neck, leaning his head forward, rolling it this way and that.

Whatever it was, it had the police now. At least, it had these two policemen.

David felt invisible walls closing in around him.

"Your dinner's been ready for nearly two hours," Mom said as they went into the kitchen. "It's warming in the oven."

"Thanks, Mom," Dad replied, "but I'm really not very hungry."

"Okay, fine," she muttered angrily, going to the

oven to turn it off. "I keep it for two hours and you don't want it."

"Sorry," he said, but he didn't seem to mean it. He stepped up behind her and touched her back. "You know, Mom, it sure is beautiful up there over the hill. Why don't we take a walk up there after you finish the dishes?"

David couldn't listen anymore; he couldn't be in the same room with his dad. He left the kitchen and sat at the foot of the stairs, chewing on a knuckle. Their words were still clear, though.

"George, you're acting very strange. Are you sure there's nothing wrong?"

"Overworked. Under a lot of pressure. Let's do the dishes and go for that walk. I could use the exercise and . . . we can talk."

No! David's mind screamed. *Don't go with him! That's what he wants! What it wants!*

"Okay," Mom said. "Just let me go to the bathroom first."

David heard her footsteps in the hall and he dashed from the stairs to stop her.

"Mom!" he whispered sharply. "I gotta talk to you!"

"Honey, can it wait? I've got to go to—"

"No, Mom, it *can't!*"

She stopped and touched his forehead. "David, you're sweating. Do you have a fever?"

"Mom, please . . . don't go over the hill. *Please!*"

"Why not, David? What's wrong?"

He clutched her hand pleadingly. "Mom, something terrible happened to Dad up there. I don't know what, but *something*. He got a scratch on his neck and now . . . now he's not Dad anymore! And it got the chief and Officer Kenney, I know it did, just now, out there!" His throat began to feel thick and tears stung his eyes. His sweaty palms were sticky against his mom's cool skin as he held her hand in both of his. "Mom, please don't go over the hill, *please!*"

"You feel okay, David?"

"*No!* I'm scared! For you!"

She squatted down, face to face with him, and touched his cheek. "Look, honey, there's nothing over that hill. The police even said so."

"What's wrong?"

David started at his dad's voice. It had that deep, throaty sound it got when Dad caught him doing something wrong.

"It's his nightmare," Mom said, standing. "He still hasn't gotten over it."

Dad sucked his cheeks in thoughtfully as he studied David. "He'll get over it." He turned to Mom. "Come on, let's get going." He put his arm around her.

"Mom . . ." David whimpered helplessly.

"It's late," she said. "Go to bed, honey." She disappeared in the bathroom and, once again, David was left alone with his dad.

Dad suddenly seemed taller than he ever had before. He held his arms a few inches from his sides, as if he might strike out at any moment.

David shrank away from him slowly.

"Go to bed—" Dad's lips pulled back over his teeth in a sneer and his voice became mocking and malicious, "*—honey.*"

At that moment, David realized he was a threat to whatever his dad had become, and the man was only biding his time until he could silence him, waiting for the right moment to take him over the hill . . . to others like him . . . to whatever David had seen go down there in the early hours of morning.

David shot up the stairs, ran to his room and slammed the door.

For a while, David thumbed through comic books and magazines, unable to read, just skimming the pictures. His guts were churning and his hands trembled slightly. He couldn't imagine feeling more helpless.

From the kitchen, sounds of dishes clattering and pans banging together let David know that his mom was still in the house loading the dishwasher, still safe. Keeping his attention trained on the noise, he undressed and put on his pajamas.

The bed felt good; Mom had put on fresh sheets that day. But David knew he couldn't sleep. He watched Jasper for a while, crawling slowly over his bark.

The kitchen was silent.

David listened hard but heard nothing. He got up and went to his door, opened it a crack, and listened. There was no one downstairs. He hurried to the window.

With an arm draped around her, his head leaning close to hers, Dad was escorting Mom up the trail, over the hill.

David opened the window and could hear, faintly, his mom's laughter on the soft breeze. His heart stopped, his blood ran cold as they neared the top of Copper Hill. He opened his mouth to scream at her, to plead with her to come back, to get away from him; he wanted her to know that wasn't really Dad, that it was someone—*something*—that only wanted to hurt her.

All that came from David's mouth was a faint, withered sound that formed one word: "Mom . . ."

David put his eye to the telescope as his dad playfully kissed Mom's cheek, making her laugh again. They stopped at the crest of the hill and Dad took her hand as he pointed toward the sand pit, apparently directing her attention to something. Then, as they started over the top, Dad turned . . . looked directly at David . . . and waved.

"*Maaawwwm!*" David screamed, much louder this time, an anguished cry that tore itself from his chest painfully. He lifted his head above the telescope and watched through burning tears as they disappeared over the hill.

She wouldn't be the same when she got back, he *knew* it. His parents were gone, both of them now, taken from him by . . . something. He folded his arms on the windowsill, leaned his head on them, and sobbed.

"Was that David?" Ellen asked, turning an ear toward the house. Just over the top of the hill, she thought she'd heard the boy's voice.

"No," George said. "Just a dog barking."

He led her down to the embankment and they stood at the edge, hand in hand, looking out over the white pool of sand. It gleamed in the moonlight, speckled here and there with shadows created by the miniature sand dunes.

"I'm a little worried about David," Ellen said.

"Don't. He'll be fine."

"You always say that, George. What if he isn't fine. He was worried all evening about you. He somehow tied your absence to his nightmare last night. I don't remember seeing him so scared."

"It'll pass, Ellen. Believe me." He sounded certain.

"Tell you the truth, babe, I've been a little worried about you, too."

"Me?" He smirked at her, giving her a sidelong look.

"Yes. You haven't really been yourself. Feeling okay?"

"Healthy as a bear."

"Anything wrong at work?"

"Oh, you know . . . the usual."

"Is that why you didn't go today?" She paid close attention to his reaction. He didn't look at her and she prompted, "Hmm?"

"I told you I had that meeting with Ed."

"All day?"

"It took some preparation."

She turned to him fully, still holding his hand, and said, "Honey, no one at the base had any idea where you were."

"Not everyone knew about it," he replied, reaching behind his neck and rubbing his fingers back and forth, rolling his head right and left.

"How's the cut on your neck?"

He smiled briefly. "Fine."

"Let me see it."

"Really, it's fine. C'mon, let's go down onto the sand." He tugged her toward the pit.

Pulling back, Ellen said, "No, I'd rather not."

"How come?"

"Oh, I just don't want to get sand in my shoes, track it into the house. . . ."

He chuckled deeply. "You never used to worry about that." He stepped forward and put his arms around her and touched his nose to hers. "Remember that night the first week we lived here? When we came down here and chased each other on the sand? And then . . . I caught you." He chuckled again, but this time it seemed different. Ellen knew it was meant to sound playful, but it seemed cold . . . unfamiliar.

"I think I'd like to go back now," she said, pulling away from him.

"Oh, come on. Just a little walk on the sand. C'mon." He held her hand firmly and pulled, smiling all the while, a stiff smile, rather forced.

Mom, please don't go over the hill, please!

The memory of David's words was like an annoying gnat flying around her ear and, just as she would a gnat, Ellen brushed it away, thinking, *That boy's imagination is starting to rub off on me.*

"Okay," she said and laughed. "For a while. I'd like to get to bed soon."

They stumbled down the embankment and onto the soft sand and suddenly, George was lunging for her, growling, "Gonna getcha!"

Giggling like a girl, Ellen ran from him, her feet pushing weakly against the sand, kicking it up behind her. She ran halfway across the pit and spun around to surprise George.

He was gone.

"George?" she said. Then she called his name loudly, looking around. He was nowhere in sight.

An owl hooted, startling her.

A bat flew quickly and softly overhead.

"George, this isn't funny. Where are you?"

She turned all the way around, scanning the pit for some sign of her husband. Nothing.

"All right, *fine*," she muttered, starting for the embankment, feeling angry and foolish for having fallen for his trick. She heard something behind her and turned. She could see nothing.

It happened again. A soft, whispery sound.

"Geor—"

Everything began to spin and the world beneath her fell away, sucking her down with it like a riptide and her arms flew upward, her hair fluttered out around her head and she opened her mouth to scream, but it never came. Her last thought was of her son:

Dear God, he was right!

David wasn't sure how long they were gone because he hadn't looked at his clock. He'd been lying on his bed sobbing, trying to think but unable to hold onto any thoughts, as if they'd been made slippery by his tears.

The back door slammed. . . .

Footsteps crossed the kitchen. . . .

There was movement in the living room. . . .

The hitching in David's chest stopped and fear dried his tears quickly as he heard their voices on the stairs, coming closer:

". . . late now . . ."

". . . yes . . ."

". . . in his room . . . ?"

They were outside the bedroom door. David's eyes flew to the knob and he slapped a hand over his mouth when he realized he hadn't locked it!

"Tomorrow," Dad said quietly. "Midnight."

"Yes, midnight," Mom agreed. "Is he asleep?"

There was silence as they listened at the door.

"Probably."

"Shouldn't we take him tonight?"

The knob turned, the door began to open, and David disappeared beneath the covers, trembling, as he had that morning.

He recognized the heaviness of Dad's footsteps walking into the room, heard a tinkly sound, like coins . . . his pennies?

The footsteps retreated, the door closed, and the voices faded down the hall.

"Tomorrow," Dad said again. "Midnight."

After he heard their door close, David sat up in his bed, pushing the covers away, and looked at his desk.

His penny collection was gone.

Chapter Seven

The next morning, after a sleepless night, David reluctantly entered the kitchen. Mom was at the stove cooking breakfast and humming. When David walked in, Mom smiled over her shoulder. As he seated himself at the table, he looked at her carefully, studying her neck. It was covered by a high collar and he could see nothing. But he was sure it was there, the little cut, the patch of bruised flesh.

The window was open and birds sang in the sun outside, as if nothing at all were wrong, as if this were a morning just like any other.

Mom put a plate of toast on the table and David nibbled at it without tasting it at all.

Dad walked in and sat down silently, watching David across the table. Unable to look at the cold eyes for long, David stared down at his toast, tore a piece in half, and removed the crust.

"Aren't you hungry, David?" Mom asked, coming

to the table with a plate of bacon. When she put it down, David stared at it in disbelief.

Black, shriveled pieces of bacon were stacked on the plate, smoke rising slowly above them.

Mom plucked a piece from the plate and took a bite, chewing it with relish.

"Are you feeling all right?" she asked him as she crunched.

Without taking his eyes from David, Dad took a piece and began eating, too.

"I don't think he's feeling well, George," Mom said, opening the refrigerator. She rummaged through it curiously, looking from one shelf to the next. Taking out a six pack of beer, she considered it a moment, then put it on the counter and grabbed a package of raw hamburger.

David watched her as the refrigerator door slowly swung closed. Mom didn't even *like* beer!

She scooped out a mound of the burger and pressed it between her hands, then grabbed the salt shaker and held it over the patty, letting the salt pour from the little holes until the raw meat was caked with a layer of white.

"I have an idea," she said, turning to them again. She pinched off a piece of burger and popped it into her mouth, talking as she chewed. "Let's all go on a picnic, up on the hill!" She smiled, still chewing.

David began to breathe fast with fear as he watched his mom's mouth, tiny lumps of raw hamburger clinging to her lips, and he wanted to speak, to ask her what she was *doing!* But he couldn't.

"Sounds like a plan," Dad said flatly.

"But, Mom," David said slowly, with effort, "you've got classes."

"We'll go this afternoon," she went on, eating another piece, ignoring David. "It's beautiful up there. Your father showed me a place last night . . . a place you've never seen before."

"Mom . . . is this a joke?"

"We'll have a great time," Dad said and smiled, eating more bacon.

"I'll pack us a lunch." Mom pulled the tab on a beer can. "Hamburgers! How does that sound? You always like that, don't you."

"But . . . I've got *school* today."

She waved her hand in dismissal. "You can miss. You don't have to go every day."

A rock-hard lump began to form in David's throat as he stood, swallowing hard to get rid of it, praying for the bus to come so he could go.

"I don't want to go," he said quietly.

"Sure you do," Dad said. "We aren't together enough. We're a family. We should do things together more. Don't you think so, Ellen?"

"That's right, George. We should be closer."

"Hey, little guy," Dad said, "give your mom a hug."

David started to move away from the table, toward the doorway out of the kitchen, but Mom stepped in front of him. He felt as if he might throw up as he tucked his thumbs under the straps of his backpack.

The bus honked its horn outside.

David felt dizzy with relief. "I gotta go," he said.

Mom glanced out the window at the bus, then looked back at David, her face determined. "Don't you want to give your mom a hug?" she asked with a tight smile.

David continued toward the doorway, saying, "My bus is here."

Mom put her beer down and stepped toward him. Before he could go around her, she grabbed his shoulders, squatted clumsily, and wrapped her arms around him, holding him close.

Chips of ice ran through David's veins. This was not a hug his mother would give him. It was cold, clutching, possessive. He trembled in her arms and did not return the hug; his head was on her shoulder, against her neck, and his eyes moved to the spot just below her head, knowing what was there even though he was unable to see it. With a sudden jerk, he pulled away from her and saw the look in her eyes. She looked, for a moment, like a cat about to pounce.

David turned and ran as fast as he could from the house.

George and Ellen Gardiner followed David out of the house. They walked slowly down the drive as he boarded the bus.

"I told you we should have taken him last night," Ellen said impatiently. "He's becoming a problem."

George squinted in the morning sun. They stopped at the end of the drive. Shaking his head slightly, George said, "No. Everything will be fine."

As the bus drove away loudly, George raised a hand and waved with a smile. When it was gone, he looked at Ellen.

"Midnight," he said quietly.

At recess, David sat alone at the jungle gym, gazing through the bars like a prisoner. He certainly felt like a prisoner, alone and trapped.

On the bus, David had tried to tell Doug about the

UFO he'd seen, about his parents' frightening behavior, and the cuts and everything. But Doug had only laughed.

"I never thought I'd say this to anybody," Doug had said and chuckled, "but maybe you've been reading too many comic books!"

David had stopped talking then, realizing *no one* was going to believe him. He was on his own.

As he sat on the jungle gym, he stared at the cut on his hand. He'd taken the Band-Aid off in the shower. A scab had formed; the cut was healing. Why didn't the cut on his dad's neck heal? What was it and who had put it there?

And what did they want with David's pennies . . . ?

David started at the skull-splitting slam and turned to see Doug pounding his baseball bat on tne jungle gym.

"Hey," Doug said, tilting his head and squinting, "you weren't shittin' me about that spaceship crap, were you? I mean, you're . . . well, you're pretty upset."

"Just forget it, okay?" David turned from him.

"Y'know, all the guys think you're really spaced."

"Great."

"You sure you don't wanna play?"

David shook his head. "Nah."

"Okay." Doug ran across the playground, stopped, turned back to David, and shouted, "Hey, why don't we go fly on our bikes this afternoon, huh?" Laughing, he rounded the corner of the school building to the baseball field in back.

David stood and walked slowly across the playground, his hands in his pockets, his toes scuffing the pavement. Children played around him, throwing balls, jumping rope, laughing. As he watched them, he wondered how long it would be before this thing had them, had everyone in the school . . . in the whole *town*.

He went into the building and wandered down the empty hall toward his locker. When he rounded a corner, he spotted Mrs. McKeltch down the hall, just outside her classroom, talking with the chief. He quickly ducked back around the corner, out of sight, cocked an ear, and listened.

"Midnight," the chief said.

"No problem." He heard Mrs. McKeltch open her door as the chief's footsteps faded down the hall.

Peeking around the corner, David spotted the chief disappearing through the side exit. He looked all around; he was alone. Walking on tiptoe, David went to Mrs. McKeltch's room and silently peeked in the open door.

She was standing at the blackboard, her back to him, writing something. She dropped the chalk in its tray after a moment and went into her office.

When David saw what she'd written, he stifled a gasp:

2:00 P.M. FIELD TRIP

"*That's* how they're gonna get us," David breathed.

The students always looked forward to field trips, despite the watchful presence of Mrs. McKeltch. But this one would be like no other—this would be their last. When they came back, they would be different; they would no longer be his classmates. Doug would no longer be his friend! Even Kevin would be different, changed into something . . . something *wrong*. Kevin was a dick head, but David preferred *that* to what he would become.

Mrs. McKeltch had moved the frogs into her office; there were still a few live ones left over from yesterday's dissection and David could hear them croaking. Through the doorway of her office, David could see her back. She was doing something at her desk.

Cautiously, he walked into the room and headed for her open office door, squinting at her neck. Was that . . . ? When he was just a few feet from the door, he could see a Band-Aid on her neck. Goose flesh crawled over David's shoulders. Mrs. McKeltch was bad enough already, but now . . .

"What are you doing, David?"

David whirled around to face Heather. She stood in the doorway, fists clenched, eyes cold, and he knew in an instant that they had her.

"Heather . . ." David said in a fearful whisper.

Hearing a sound behind him, he turned toward Mrs. McKeltch and his mouth fell open as he staggered backward away from her.

Mrs. McKeltch stood in her office glaring at him with wide, threatening eyes. The back end of a frog hung from her mouth, its legs kicking as she struggled to suck it in, at the same time moving toward him. She tossed her head back with a jerk, gulped loudly, and the frog disappeared, making an ugly lump in her throat and leaving a glistening slime on her lips.

Nearly tripping over desks, David dashed toward the door.

"Stop!" Mrs. McKeltch called, her voice still wet and gurgly from the frog she'd eaten. "David Gardiner!"

David raised his arm and knocked Heather out of his way, running into the hall.

"Stop right where you are!" Mrs. McKeltch roared, her heavy shoes clumping on the floor as she hurried after him.

"Linda!" David screamed as he neared her office. "Ms. Magnuson, *help!"*

Linda opened her door and stuck out her head. When she saw David running toward her, she stepped into the hall and said, "David, what's *wrong?"*

Please," he gasped, grabbing her arm.

"I've had it with you!" Mrs. McKeltch was bearing down on him, reaching out her hands.

Linda stepped between them and faced Mrs. McKeltch firmly.

"What's the problem, Mrs. McKeltch?" she asked.

"I've *told* you—" She stabbed an accusing finger toward David, who was peeking around Linda's side. "—this boy is trouble! He must be severely punished." She spoke so venomously, bits of spittle flew from her mouth. She lunged toward David, taking a swipe at him.

Linda moved quickly, cutting Mrs. McKeltch off.

"David," the nurse said softly, turning to him, "what's wrong?"

David started to reply, but Mrs. McKeltch interrupted.

"He knocked over a defenseless little girl!" she snapped. "And he was prying, the little snoop!"

"Please, Mrs. McKeltch," Linda said, "let me talk to him."

"No!" She held out a hand, her fingers curved slightly, resembling claws. "Give him to *me!"*

Doors were opening and other teachers were peering down the hall toward them. When Mrs. McKeltch noticed them, she relaxed a bit.

"Please," Linda said again, quieter now, "let me talk to him. David, come into my office."

David stepped inside, glad to be away from Mrs. McKeltch. He turned and looked through the doorway as the teacher leaned toward Linda, clenching her teeth and trembling with anger.

"You're pushing it, sister!" Mrs. McKeltch hissed. "I'll be back for him in five minutes." She turned and stalked down the hall, calling behind her, "Five minutes!"

Linda came inside, closed the door, and sighed.

David was pacing the floor, his fingers wiggling nervously at his sides, his eyes wide with fear.

"David, David," Linda said gently, "relax. It's okay. Just relax."

"But you don't understand!" David panted.

"What? Understand what?" She took his hand and led him to a chair. "Sit down, David, and tell me. What don't I understand?"

He sat in the chair and stared at her, fidgeting, his mouth open.

Leaning on her desk and facing him, Linda said, "David, whatever you tell me stays in this room."

David searched her face for a hint of deception, wanting desperately to trust her, but afraid to take that chance. There was only one way he could tell for sure. . . .

"You know, I'm here to help, David," she assured him with a smile. "I mean, I'm a nurse and I'm supposed to say that, I know, but I mean it. I really do."

David chewed his lip, looking into her eyes. Her smile seemed genuine, heartfelt, but still . . .

He took in a deep breath. "First . . . can I see the back of your neck?"

Linda's eyebrows rose in surprise. "The back of my . . ." Puzzled, she turned her head and lifted her shiny blond hair from her shoulders.

Perfect, unblemished white skin.

David was so happy he almost laughed.

"All right," he said.

David's story went on longer than she'd expected. He spoke fast, gesturing with his hands, his eyes wide and his body tense. She had to slow him down a few times, but it never worked. Linda tried hard to look attentive and not register the amusement she was feeling, tried not to look as if he were telling her a joke. When he finally got to the frog's legs hanging out of Mrs. McKeltch's mouth, she could not stifle a giggle.

"Eating a frog?" she asked.

He nodded.

"Well," she sighed. She leaned forward, rubbing her thighs absently, trying to choose her words carefully. "I don't know, David. That's some story. You realize that, don't you?"

"It's not a story!"

Be understanding, she thought. "A UFO lands in back of your house and puts something in your dad's and mom's necks, then gets the police and your teacher and your friend Heather and her father and . . ." She shook her head slowly, thinking about his tale for a second. "How did it get Mrs. McKeltch?" she asked with a frown.

"She said the frogs came from Copper Hill. She must've gone there and . . . they got her."

She sat up straight on the desk, locked her elbows, and pressed her palms down on the edge of the desktop.

He looked so sincere, so desperate to be believed.

"David," she said, "I want to believe you. I really do, but—"

"Then why don't you?" David asked so forcefully that it almost brought him to his feet.

"It's just so farfetched. Not that I don't believe in UFOs, because I do."

"You *do?*"

"Well . . ." She hesitated, wondering if she should have said that. If she told him about the thing she'd seen in the sky one night six years ago, he might even be more upset if she disbelieved his story. But, having brought it up, she decided to go on. "It was late at night. I was driving back after an evening with friends. This was in Oregon several years ago. I saw this light over the highway, slowed down, and looked out the window and I saw this . . . I don't know, *something* up in the sky." She shrugged.

"What'd it look like?"

"Like a . . . well, a glowing Brillo pad," she said and laughed. "But David, what would you think if someone told you the story you've just told me?"

"I've believe him!" he said without hesitation.

"You would, huh? And why is that?"

David sat forward in his chair, put his hand over hers, and squeezed. " 'Cause he wouldn't lie," he said earnestly.

His face was full of energy; his lips twitched, his

nostrils flared, his eyes narrowed, widened, and narrowed again. He seemed to be willing her to believe him.

Someone knocked hard on the door. "Miss Magnuson?" It was Mrs. McKeltch.

"It's on her neck," David whispered to Linda, jerking his head toward the door. "You can see for yourself."

"Stay here a minute," Linda said, crossing the office and going out into the hall.

"Well?" Mrs. McKeltch said, her arms folded.

"Mrs. McKeltch," Linda said and smiled, "David seems concerned about a . . . an injury to your neck."

The teacher pulled her head back suspiciously and looked down her nose at Linda. "My neck?"

"He says you have a bandage on it."

Lifting her hand, Mrs. McKeltch pressed her fingers to the back of her neck. "Well, yes. I . . . I have a boil on my neck."

"Why don't you let me take a look at it," Linda said kindly, taking a step toward her. "I might be able to help you clear it up." She reached her hand toward the woman's neck.

"Don't you touch me!" Mrs. McKeltch barked, jerking away from Linda.

Her words were so sharp—sharp even for Mrs. McKeltch—that Linda flinched.

"I want the boy," Mrs. McKeltch said softly, venomously.

"But maybe I can—"

"Never mind my neck! I want David Gardiner!" She tried to move around Linda toward the office, but Linda stepped in front of the door and stood her ground.

Mrs. McKeltch's lips pulled back over her yellow teeth and with quiet malice, she said, "If you don't give him to me . . ."

Linda stared her down, folding her arms as if to say, *I'm not going anywhere.*

Mrs. McKeltch turned and stormed down the hall, yelling behind her, "You've got a lot of nerve, sister!"

What a bitch! Linda thought with amazement. It was hard for her to believe the woman had managed to stay in the teaching profession so long.

"Ms. Magnuson!"

Linda recognized the breathy, perky voice and turned to greet Mr. Cross.

"Is David Gardiner with you?" he asked.

Linda suddenly felt very suspicious of everyone around her. After all, David had been right about Mrs. McKeltch's neck. And if it were really just a boil, why would the teacher be so reluctant to let Linda look at it.

"What if he were . . . ?" Linda asked, cocking a brow.

The tall man blinked. "I beg your pardon?"

"I'm sorry," she said, chiding herself for making such a foolish remark. "Yes, he's with me."

"Oh, dear. Well, anyhow, his father is on the phone and wants to talk to you."

"Oh. Okay." She pushed the door open and headed for the phone. She felt David's hand on her arm and turned, looking down at his worried face.

"Don't tell them anything I said," he whispered.

"Hello, this is Linda Magnuson," she said pleasantly, looking down at David with curious eyes, as if to ask, *What's going on here, David?*

"I understand that you have my son in your office," Mr. Gardiner said sternly.

"Yes, I do. How did you know?"

"What's he doing there?"

She glanced at David again. "He's upset. We were just having a little talk."

"Just a little talk . . ." He sounded slightly mocking. "About *what?*"

"Well, he, uh . . . he seems to be under some kind of stress." *Jesus,* she thought, *how did I get into this?*

David leaned forward in his chair and buried his face in his palms.

"What has he told you?" Mr. Gardiner asked.

That seemed, to Linda, a rather odd question. As if he had something to hide.

"Um, look, Mr. Gardiner, I don't—"

"You people have a lot of nerve, meddling into family affairs like this."

"I'm not meddling, Mr. Gardiner, really. I'm just trying to help your son. He says—"

"No. I don't want to hear it. His storytelling has gotten him into a lot of trouble."

Mrs. Gardiner spoke up on another line: "The boy's got quite an imagination. We had to take him to a psychiatrist last year."

"Oh?" Linda said, her face relaxing. "A psychiatrist. I didn't know that."

David's head shot up, his mouth gaping, and he stood, shaking his head frantically.

"He needs professional help," Mrs. Gardiner said coldly.

Linda was alarmed at her tone and the remark about the psychiatrist was immediately forgotten. Mrs. Gardiner sounded as if she were speaking of a total stranger, not her son, perhaps a killer she'd read about in the paper.

"Actually," Linda said uncertainly, "I think—"

"I'm not particularly interested, Miss Magnuson, in what you *think*. My wife and I are going away on a business trip this afternoon and we want David with us. Keep him in your office until we arrive. We'll be right there."

"Of course, no—"

He hung up.

"—problem."

Linda replaced the receiver slowly, almost afraid to look at David. When she did, he stepped toward her and breathed, "Well?"

"They're coming to pick you up."

"No!" he shrieked. "I won't go with them!" His voice was shrill with panic.

"David, I told them I'd keep you here. I can't just—"

"No! Let me outta here!" He turned and started for the door, but Linda caught his arm before he could get away.

"David, please, just sit down."

"Oh, God," he groaned, sinking into the chair, near tears, "you're on their side."

"Oh, boy," she sighed, running a hand through her hair. "This is going to be a mess."

Back at the school where she'd worked in Oregon, nothing like this had ever happened. She'd gotten along well with the students, the faculty, and all the parents. Her salary hadn't been any less than it was at Menzies. Everything had always gone smoothly. She suddenly hadn't the slightest idea why she'd left. She sat down behind her desk and studied David.

His nose was red and he was sniffling frequently to keep from crying.

"Please," he whispered, "don't let them take me."

Something was wrong, whatever it was.

"Okay," she said quietly. "You can go out the window."

He stood, beaming, and hurried toward her, as if to hug her, but only stood across the desk, grinning. "Thank you so much!" He bounded toward the window.

"Wait a sec," Linda said, grabbing her purse and fishing through it for her key. She decided that, if she was going to get involved with whatever was happening, she was going to be responsible about it. "Here," she said, handing the key to David. "This opens my back door. I'll meet you there after school."

He put the key in his pocket and went to the window, lifted the sash, and hopped onto the sill. As he swung a leg outside, a bag of M&M's fell out of his backpack.

"Here," Linda said, picking them up. "Don't forget these."

"Thanks." Gratitude warmed his face as he stuffed the bag into his pack, then lowered himself out the window. Seconds later, he poked his head back in.

"What is it?" Linda asked.

"Where do you live?"

"Oh, uh . . ." She scratched her cheek. She could never remember her new address when she needed it.

"*Where?*" David prompted.

"Um, I just moved and I don't . . . uh, it's, uh—"

The door flew open and David ducked back out the window.

"Where's David?" Heather demanded.

Linda had never heard a child use such a cold tone. "He's not feeling well, Heather," she said, trying not to sound guilty. "Why don't you . . . come back later."

"Well . . ." Heather's nose scrunched up, as if she were frustrated. "All right. But if you see him . . . tell him I'm looking for him."

As the girl turned her back and left, Linda saw, underneath her bobbing ponytail, a small X-shaped bandage and, beneath that, a tiny trickle of dried blood.

My god, Linda thought with a chill.

She stood, rushed to the door, and closed it, then returned to the window.

"I'm on South Arroyo," she said quickly. "Four two . . . six . . . no, *no!* It's four-six-two South Arroyo!"

"Bye!"

"Do you know how to get there?" she asked him nervously, sticking her head out the window.

"Yeah! I'll find you." Then, under his breath, he said, "Before they find me, I hope."

When he was gone, Linda closed the window and dropped into her chair with a deep sigh. She sat at her desk and rubbed her eyes for a moment, then stood, deciding to get a cup of tea from the faculty lounge. She walked down the hall hoping to avoid Mrs. McKeltch.

Seconds before she reached the lounge, an angry voice behind her said, "Where's my son?"

She turned to face Mr. and Mrs. Gardiner. They stood side by side, very straight, and both looked upset, preoccupied.

"I'm sorry," Linda said slowly, trying to come up with an excuse. "I was out of my office for a minute and when I got back—" She shrugged. "—he was gone."

"He's not well," Mrs. Gardiner said with little concern in her voice.

"He may be in danger," David's father said through tight lips. He stepped forward angrily. "We'll sue, you know. What the hell kind of nurse are you, anyway?" He paused, as if waiting for an answer, then said, "What did he talk to you about?"

"He was upset about . . . he's having a problem with one of his teachers. That's all."

"I *told* you," Mrs. Gardiner said, "he needs psychiatric help." She did not sound worried; she sounded impatient.

"Is that all he said?" Mr. Gardiner asked.

"Yes." She nodded and tried to smile convincingly. "It was just a small problem with one of his teachers. That's all. I'm sure you have nothing to worry about."

The parents glanced at one another, then brushed by Linda, as if she weren't even there.

Jesus, Linda thought as she went into the lounge, *some people should not be allowed to have children.*

David crouched behind the bushes outside Linda's window for a while, peering through the branches at the parking lot and playground. The students had all returned to class and the grounds were deserted.

Moving through the bushes, he hugged the wall as he made his way toward the lot and the front gate. Looking around once more and seeing no one, he made a run for it, cautiously weaving through the parked cars. He came to a van and stopped a moment, pressing himself against the side.

Footsteps! David tensed and waited.

"I couldn't see him, but he's there. She's hiding him, I think."

Heather! David looked around the front corner of the van. She was headed straight for him. But who was she talking to?

He went around to the back of the van. Its door was ajar and, giving no thought to the possible consequences, David opened it and got inside, half closing it behind him. When he turned around, he almost screamed.

He was face to face with a skeleton! He clamped his hand over his mouth, breathing hard through his nose as he looked around him.

The bulging eyes of dead reptiles gazed at him from Mason jars.

Stuffed rodents stood frozen in lifelike positions.

Colorful butterflies were mounted on cardboard.

He suddenly realized whose van it was, and he felt weak all over. Looking out the small round window in the side of the van, he saw the back of her head through the tinted glass: gray hair in sharp waves and tight curls, a matronly collar trimmed with lace. He scrunched down in the van listening to the beat of his heart.

"He's still with the nurse, I'm sure of it," Heather said outside.

"His parents will take him," Mrs. McKeltch told her with assurance.

He couldn't stay. Leaving would mean being seen, but staying in the van was too dangerous. He lunged for the door just as it was slammed hard from the outside. David turned and faced the death cluttered all around him. Quietly, he crawled toward the front of the van and curled up behind the jump seats.

The door on the driver's side opened and the van shook slightly as someone got in. David softly sniffed the air.

Mothballs.

He closed his eyes tightly and prayed that Mrs. McKeltch wouldn't—

She started the van, backed out of the space, and drove from the parking lot.

Chapter Eight

A burning ache began to spread from David's lower back as the van rolled over a bumpy road. The ride had been smooth for a while, but Mrs. McKeltch had turned onto a twisty, bumpy road that jostled him mercilessly. His whole body had been tensed since the ride began and he would have given anything to stretch out and relax. But he feared being discovered; his blood chilled at the thought of what Mrs. McKeltch would do if she found him.

David shifted his position slightly, trying to sit up more. His arm slipped and his hand hit something cold, something that rattled loudly, making him wince. He looked down at the floor and found a stack of copper piping beside him.

Copper? he thought, remembering his missing penny collection.

He remained stiff as stone, waiting for a reaction

from Mrs. McKeltch. When none came, he decided she hadn't noticed the sound. Moving just a fraction of an inch at a time, David sat up a bit more, just enough to carefully peek over the back of the seat.

Mrs. McKeltch sat rigidly at the wheel, her eyes locked on the road. The bandage on the back of her neck had come loose and was dangling over her collar, revealing a reddened, bruised spot with black stitches holding together an X-shaped cut.

David wondered what was beneath that cut, what had been put into her neck.

Through the window, David saw that the van was driving on an old road that led through the woods. The area looked familiar; Dad had brought him out here once for a Sunday ride.

Mrs. McKeltch drove off the road and stopped, then turned off the ignition and got out.

When he was certain she wouldn't see him, David leaned over the back of the seat and looked out the window. Mrs. McKeltch walked around the trees, fast as always, looking as if she were on her way to oversee a hanging. She stopped at a hillside, facing what looked like a tunnel. She stood at the hole for a while, staring into the darkness, then she disappeared inside, swallowed up by the ground.

David quickly crawled over the seat and got out on the passenger side, shutting the door with a quiet click. He jogged through the woods to the hillside and stopped at the mouth of the tunnel.

The opening was about eight feet tall and too round to be natural; it had been cut into the hill.

David looked around him, taking a deep breath of the fresh air, and watched a squirrel shimmy up a tree.

I could run now, he thought. *I'd be a lot safer if I made tracks outta here.*

But he knew that whatever had taken possession of his parents, whatever had put those cuts in their necks, was somewhere in that tunnel and Mrs. McKeltch would lead him to it if he followed her.

He could still hear the crunch of her footsteps as she went deeper into the tunnel. Walking softly, David went inside, his heart pounding in his throat.

Leaving the daylight behind, David found that the tunnel wasn't as dark inside as he'd expected. An orange-hued light, dim at first, grew brighter as he followed the sound of Mrs. McKeltch's heavy shoes.

The tunnel was perfectly rounded and formed by spiraled ridges, as if a giant screw had pushed through the earth. Up ahead, it curved to the right. Keeping a good distance between himself and Mrs. McKeltch, David waited till she'd rounded the bend before continuing.

He followed her through the long, quiet tunnel, which occasionally wound in S-shaped curves, until, around one of the corners, he watched her approach a large wishbone-shaped archway that was even bigger than the mouth of the tunnel. Pausing only for a brief moment, she went through, still walking fast, her nose in the air as if she not only knew where she was going but had good reason to go there.

David went to the archway and gingerly touched its side; it was smooth and cool, a bit moist. There was a gap between the archway and the tunnel. It was separate from the tunnel . . . something very large and flush with the opening. . . .

The ship! David thought. This was what he'd seen

from his bedroom window, lowering through the storm clouds!

David took in a deep, steadying breath, let it out slowly, and stepped through the archway.

He blanched at the smell, which hit him hard. The air was humid and thick with a wet, almost dirty odor. Something vaguely familiar about it made him search his memory. Where had he smelled it before? When? He couldn't remember.

There was a strange light in the ship. It seemed to have no one origin; it came from everywhere. As he entered, it changed from a soft gold to a darker, deep orange.

Mrs. McKeltch was ascending a ribbed, spiral ramp. It looked as if it had been made of big bones lying crossways, but they weren't bones. David wanted to bend down and touch them, but he didn't have time; he didn't want to lose Mrs. McKeltch.

The walls had a dull, opalescent glow that reflected the constantly changing light. No matter what the color, he noticed, there was always a flat greenish tint to the walls.

Once Mrs. McKeltch had rounded the first curve of the spiral ramp, David started after her, moving slowly as he studied the walls around him. They glistened with moisture. Jagged, raised lines on the walls throbbed gently, forming patterns that made him think of a map with the roads all embossed. They looked like . . . David touched one of them and jerked his hand back. Veins! They were veins, gushing with warm fluid. He pressed a palm to the wall; it was firm but pliant, warm and vibrating slightly, silently. When he pulled his hand away, it was sticky with a fine sheen of mucus. He lifted it to his nose, sniffed, and frowned.

It smelled vaguely of copper, like a wet gunny sack filled with dirty old pennies.

A burst of steam shot upward near his feet and he nearly fell over it jumping away. There was a hole at the bottom of the wall, like a small crater, or . . .

Jeez, David thought, wiping his palm on his pants, *it looks like a big rectum!*

Looking around, he discovered the holes were scattered all over the walls and along the edge of the ramp. Steam occasionally oozed or shot from them, disappearing in misty puffs.

Every few feet along the ramp, the wall opened into a dark hole, too dark for David to tell how deep. Perhaps they were tunnels . . . he couldn't tell. As he passed them slowly, he thought he sensed movement in the darkness, so he tried to keep clear of them.

Mrs. McKeltch's footsteps were silenced. David stopped and listened a moment, but he could only hear a low hum that came from somewhere in the ship.

As he rounded the next curve, he spotted Mrs. McKeltch at the top of the ramp, her back to him. She faced a massive platform; it looked like an altar or throne. It seemed made of the same hard, bonelike material upon which David walked, but it had a sort of melted or eroded look to it. Around the base of the platform, mist flowed from a seam that ran along the edge. Icy-smooth shafts, some tall and narrow, others short and squat, rose like carefully polished stalagmites around the throne. There were no sharp angles or jagged edges, only golden-hued curves that looked smooth as glass. In the very center was a raised surface, flat at the top, waiting to be occupied.

Above the throne on the back wall was a rounded panel with an S-shaped seam, like a camera lens. Mrs.

McKeltch stared at it, still and patient . . . waiting.

David spotted movement on each side of the platform, someone—or something—coming from the darkness toward Mrs. McKeltch. He looked around for a place to hide. The ramp forked just ahead of him, one path leading to Mrs. McKeltch, the other going upward slightly and around a corner. David took the inclining walkway and watched from around a corner.

When he saw the things hobbling out of the shadows to flank Mrs. McKeltch, David almost gasped aloud.

They were about eight feet tall and sort of round, bobbing up and down on long bony legs. Their skin looked thick and fell in folds around their flat, piglike noses. Their eyes were big, with smooth, bulbous ridges over the top, like a toad's eyes. The flesh around the eyes and nose was speckled and reptilian. The tops of their heads were bright pink and soft-looking, like an exposed organ. Their arms reached to the floor and propped them up from behind when they stood beside Mrs. McKeltch. They were never still, always bobbing . . . bobbing. . . .

The S-shaped seam on the wall above them slid open. Something moved in the darkness beyond. A head, massive and sphynxlike with small glistening eyes, began to ease its way out of the orifice.

David instinctively took a step back, partly to remain hidden and partly from revulsion at what he saw.

Its brain was exposed atop its head and sharply slanted ridges hooded the beady eyes. It slid slowly toward Mrs. McKeltch with the fluid motions of a serpent, its long round body rippling with powerful muscles that moved it along smoothly. Something dangled on its underside . . . a strip of fleshy strands like—what was the name of that stuff he'd read about in his biology book?—*cilia*.

A tentacle sprouted from mounds just below the round head on each side and ran the length of the body, disappearing into the orifice. It arched its head upward, like a cobra, and hovered there a moment looking around the throne, at Mrs. McKeltch, at the two creatures beside her. Then it lowered itself to the flat surface, coming to rest. The tentacles slithered from the hole, swung around slowly, and wrapped about the platform below the creature. It fixed its cold stare on Mrs. McKeltch.

The orange light in the chamber faded to a soft yellow, then to turquoise as something to the right caught David's eye. On one of the walls was a huge, butterfly-shaped panel. No, no, it wasn't a panel; it was a . . . membrane. The center was made of an opaque material and webbed with tiny veinlike lines. It shimmered—that's what David had seen. Small worms of light trickled along the veins and scurried over the surface.

The light changed again, this time to a soft green.

Mrs. McKeltch nodded. But the creature's mouth hadn't moved.

The membrane shimmered again, the light changed back to yellow, and Mrs. McKeltch raised her right arm.

The thing was communicating with her! It wasn't speaking, it was . . . *thinking* to her, and the changes in the light, the energy sparkling through the membrane, those were all reactions to the creature's thoughts, its commands. What was the word for it? David had read about it once in an issue of *Eerie*. Telepathy, that was it! The creature was using telepathy to communicate with Mrs. McKeltch, and it was drawing its energy from the ship. Or . . . maybe the ship was drawing its energy from the creature. . . .

Too many thoughts at once, David told himself. *Just watch for now.*

Mrs. McKeltch lowered her right arm, then lifted and lowered her left. Like a puppet on a string she raised first one leg, lowered it, then raised the other. And with each movement, David saw something sparkle on the back of her neck.

He stepped forward, craned his neck, squinted, trying to focus on the spot, the cut on her neck.

It was a thin, spiraled needle. Each time Mrs. McKeltch moved a limb, the needle spun in and out of the X-shaped cut. As her arm raised, the needle spiraled outward a bit; as the arm lowered, the needle went back into her neck. When she raised her leg, it moved out even farther, then back inward as the leg was dropped.

David stared in awe as his teacher—feared and hated on the campus of W. C. Menzies Elementary School—was tested like a new toy by the huge, slug-like creature. She was no longer the cold, unsmiling woman who could silence an entire classroom of children by counting to five. She was a marionette, a grotesque doll.

David was so pleased he almost smiled. But not before he felt hot, sticky breath on his neck. He whipped around with a gasp and found himself face to face with one of the eight-foot-tall creatures. Its huge mouth opened, jagged fangs dripping with clear fluids, and roared. It was a low, throaty, rumbly roar, wet and sloppy, and it came with a rush of fetid breath that smelled of decay. The thing lunged at David, snapping its fangs together inches before his face.

David screamed so loudly that his throat hurt. He threw himself backward from the creature, nearly losing his balance but pivoting before he could fall. As he ran down the ramp, he saw Mrs. McKeltch pointing at him with an accusing finger.

"David Gardiner!" she called, her voice echoing in the huge chamber. The light changed to a deep, bloody red.

David glanced over his shoulder and saw the thing gaining on him, moving with surprising speed, its flabby, moist skin squishing together with each movement.

The two creatures flanking Mrs. McKeltch lumbered quickly toward David, snarling, their vicious eyes locked on him like gun sights as he came down the ramp. David realized they would cut him off at the fork if he didn't hurry; he began running faster, as fast as he could, tryng not to trip on the ramp's ridges.

The two creatures were nearing the fork quickly and David knew he wasn't going to make it. Clenching his teeth, he jumped, pushing himself from the descending ramp with all his might, as if diving into home base for a homer, landing at the intersection a few seconds before the two creatures. They lurched forward, snapping their fangs at him as he scurried toward the archway on hands and knees, scrambling to get back on his feet. Once he was up, he kept running.

One of the creatures suddenly lunged out of one of the dark holes, blocking his path, its arms outstretched for him, legs spread, its mouth yawning open. Without slowing, David dropped to the ridged floor and rolled between the bony legs of the monster. A sharp pain stabbed through his left knee, making him stumble as he tried to get up again.

The bag of M&M's in his backpack slipped out and burst open on the ramp, scattering like marbles, but David didn't give it a second thought. Wincing with pain, he limped on, staggering toward the archway, passing through it and into the spiraled tunnel, heading for daylight.

At the mouth of the tunnel, he fell again and the pain went through his leg like jagged pieces of glass. He began crawling frantically, expecting to feel the razorlike teeth of one of the creatures close on him at any moment. As he scrambled toward the road, he glanced over his shoulder.

Nothing.

He paused and listened.

Back in the tunnel, he heard curious grumblings, grunts, and wheezing sounds.

David stood and faced the tunnel opening, his breath coming hard and fast, the pain in his knee almost unbearable.

What were they doing? Maybe they couldn't come out of the tunnel. Maybe they had to stay where it was dark and wet, like salamanders.

David took a few painful steps toward the tunnel and peeked around the edge of the opening. Nothing. But he could still hear them back there, murmuring like hunger pangs in a giant stomach. Cautiously, he went back into the tunnel, all the way to the curve. Pressing his back to the wall, he craned his head around toward the archway.

The four creatures were standing on the ramp, huddled over something. His M&M's! One of them scooped some of the candy up in its gnarled hand and stared at it.

They're like drones in a beehive, David thought as he watched them. They were obviously not very intelligent and seemed able to do no more than guard the ship or pursue intruders.

The creature plopped the M&M's into its huge mouth as the others watched and waited. Its fat, wet lips smacked together, an odd look came over its beady eyes as its tongue, a plump, clumsy chunk of old meat, slid back and forth the length of its mouth. Suddenly, it leaned forward and wretched, spewing the chewed-up M&M's into a sticky pile at its feet. The others stepped back, grunting.

"The boy!" Mrs. McKeltch called from within the ship. "Stop him!"

The four drones turned at once toward the archway, looking directly at David. With a soft cry of horror, David turned and ran, trying to ignore the pain in his knee. Once he was out of the tunnel again, he did not stop. He ran through the woods.

Linda's house wasn't far; in fact, it was closer than his own. He slapped through the brush, ducked branches, and dodged rocks and logs. After several minutes of running, he slowed to get his bearings. He knew the sand pit was dangerous, although he didn't know exactly why, so he wanted to stay clear of it. After a few moments, he continued, all the while casting glances over his shoulder.

Barbara Tyler was a close friend of Linda's. They'd gone to school together, both high school and college.

Still in Oregon, Barbara had a private practice as a child psychologist. Linda had spoken with her just two nights ago, but decided to call her again. She could probably shed some light on David's problem, maybe give Linda some advice. She was dialing the number when she heard a car drive up out front. She put down the phone and went to the window.

"Oh, god," she sighed when she saw the police car. They'd want to know if David were with her or if she'd seen him. She could lie her way through their questions, but what if David showed up while they were there? Linda quickly grabbed her purse and coat, her car keys from the phone table, and went to the door, slipping her arms into the sleeves. She opened the door before they could ring the bell.

"Miss Magnuson?"

"Yes." She smiled at them. Two of them; one was tall and not bad-looking, the other quite a bit older with a belly hanging over his belt.

"Chief Ward, Miss Magnuson. Willowbrook Police Department."

"What can I do for you?"

"Well; Officer Kenney and I are looking for a boy. David Gardiner. Know him?"

"Of course." She looked at both of them carefully. She recognized their names; they were the ones David had told her about. They seemed normal enough, but . . . "Has something happened to him?" she asked, feigning concern.

"Don't know, ma'am," Kenney said. "His parents can't find him. They gave us a call. He hasn't been here, has he?"

"Of course not," she said. "And I shouldn't be

here, either. I have to get to the post office before it closes and then I have to meet a friend. I'm running short of time, so—" Her best smile. "—if you don't mind, I'm going to take off."

"Ma'am," Chief Ward said. "Do you have any reason to believe the boy might be in the neighborhood?"

She shook her head and chuckled. "I said I don't know where he is. I'm the school nurse, not the resident sitter." She stepped between them onto the porch, pulled the door shut, and locked it. "Sorry I can't help you. I hope he's all right, but I really do have to go."

The policemen did not smile; they looked at one another for a moment, Chief Ward tilting his head oddly. Something had been silently communicated, Linda realized.

"Have a good day," she said, heading for her car. As she got behind the wheel, she thought, *They are pretty strange*. She started the ignition and backed out, drove down the road and around a corner, then pulled onto the shoulder and parked in a shaded area. Remaining behind the wheel, tapping her fingers thoughtfully, she whispered, "David, where are you?"

David was across the road from Linda's house, hidden in the shadows of the trees. When he'd spotted the police car, he'd hidden himself well. Linda's car was nowhere in sight and the chief and Kenney were walking up and down the street, their eyes scanning the yards in the neighborhood. He knew they were looking for him.

But where was Linda? In the house, perhaps, being

held by one of them? Had they taken her somewhere else?

Maybe they've got her in the ship, he thought. *Maybe they're putting one of those things in her—*

His thoughts were shattered as a hand reached from behind and clamped over his mouth, pulling him hard into the bushes. . . .

Chapter Nine

When David tried to scream, Linda whispered into his ear, "Quiet, David, *sshhhh!*"

David's rigid body relaxed when he knew it was only Linda and he turned around and hugged her with relief. "I found 'em!" he exclaimed breathlessly.

"David, calm down," she said, taking his hand and leading him through the woods along the edge of the road. "We're in trouble. I've parked my car down here off the road. We'll have to—"

"But I saw them!" he went on. "They were bigger than anything I've ever seen!"

She didn't seem to hear him. "God, they probably think I've kidnaped you," she muttered to herself, exasperated.

"They tried to catch me! They chased me through a tunnel! They nearly killed me!"

Linda stopped and looked down at him with concern. "What? Who?"

"Those . . . *things!* They're huge, ugly, slimy . . ." David searched his memory for something similar, something to which he could compare the drones that had chased him. "Giant Mr. Potato Heads!" he exclaimed.

"Hold it, just slow down, David, I don't understand—"

"I'll show you! You can see for yourself!" He grabbed her hand and dragged her toward her car. "Get in!"

Linda sighed as she got behind the wheel. David got in beside her, bouncing on the seat with excitement.

"C'mon, let's go!" he said.

Linda started the car and got on the road.

"David," she said softly, "tell me . . . you're not a crazy child, are you?" She quickly added, "I mean, on the phone, your parents told me you'd seen a psychiatrist, remember?"

David's heart sank. He knew it had to come up again sooner or later.

"Only a few times," he said. "I was having bad dreams every night and Mom and Dad were—turn right here—they were worried that something was wrong. So they sent me to this Dr. Wycliffe."

"Did it help?"

"No," David said pointedly. "He was crazy himself. He wore this too-pay. You know, fake hair? And he never talked to me, he just asked questions. When I asked him a question, he would just ask another question, almost like I wasn't even there, and . . . and . . ." He turned toward her, his vision blurring with tears. "Linda, please, I don't want to go back to him. Don't let them send me. I'm not crazy! I really saw this. You'll believe me when you see it!"

"Okay, okay, calm down. Just tell me how to get there."

David directed her to the opposite side of the sand pit.

"Okay, slow down here," he said. "Mrs. McKeltch might still be around."

But the van was gone. Linda parked several yards away from the spot where Mrs. McKeltch had left her van earlier and they got out. David took her hand again, hopping from one foot to the other as he tugged on her arm. "C'mon, c'mon!" He led her to the hillside, to—

The tunnel was gone.

"This is the spot!" David said, his throat clenching slightly, making his voice high and squeaky. "It was here!"

"I don't see anything," Linda said. Her voice was soft, but firm, as if her suspicions had been confirmed.

"But it was *here!* I saw it! I went inside!" He went to the side of the hill where the tunnel had been and pressed his hands to the hard, cold earth. Solid. Undisturbed. There was even grass growing from the spot that earlier had been the mouth of the tunnel. "It's gone," David whispered. He turned to Linda; she was looking at him skeptically, eyes narrow, her hands folded behind her back. "I swear it was here," he insisted, but his voice was not as forceful as before.

"But it's not, David."

He looked at the hillside again, remembering the things that had chased him, the creature that had slithered out of its hole and come to rest on its altar.

"They moved it!" David said with certainty, spinning to face Linda. "They can do that—move tunnels!"

"Oh, David, this is just too . . . crazy. It's *crazy!*"

"But you saw the Band-Aids on their necks!"

"Yes, David, but they were just Band-Aids. That's all."

"Okay. Then we have to go to the hill." He began running toward Copper Hill, toward the sand pit, without waiting for Linda. Over his shoulder, he called, "C'mon! I know a path!"

"Oh, all right," Linda sighed, hurrying to keep up with him.

They took a path that led around the pit and up Copper Hill.

"Careful," David said, panting, "they may be watching."

Trying to remain unseen, they climbed to the crest of the hill. Linda leaned against a tree, exhausted.

David turned toward his house, looking for some sign of his parents, but saw nothing. The back door was open, which was odd. But David paid it little attention; nothing was as it should be. Turning, he looked out over the sand pit. The white sand was smooth and undisturbed; it looked warm and inviting in the sun.

"Now, tell me, David," Linda said, trying to catch her breath, "does it look to you like anything landed there?"

David searched in desperation for something that would convince her, but he saw nothing. A gentle wind blew, hissing through the trees above them; fleecy white clouds moved lethargically across the blue sky.

"David," Linda said, hunching down in front of him and taking his hands, "listen to me. We're in trouble, both of us. I've helped you run away, do you understand? Now I can make up some story that will smooth things over. You could back me up."

David started to shake his head and protest, but Linda pulled him closer to her.

"Shush, listen to me. Your house is right down there. Why don't you let me take you home and tell your parents something that will calm them down? So they won't be so mad at us?" She raised her eyebrows and smiled slightly, her face kind and hopeful. "What do you say, David?"

He felt hollow inside. He'd lost her trust. She thought that he was crazy. David wanted to run, but he had nowhere to go. He wanted to make her believe him, but he had nothing to prove his claim—until he looked down the hill again at his house.

A white NASA Jeep was pulling up the driveway.

"Get down!" David warned, dropping to his knees behind a tree and pulling Linda with him. "Look."

As they watched, two men in orange jump suits got out of the Jeep. One held a detector of some sort. It looked like a metal detector, the kind people used at the beach to find coins buried in the sand.

"Those are space agency technicians," David whispered. "What are they doing here?"

The men walked toward the front door, disappearing on the other side of the house.

David and Linda watched silently, waiting.

After a few moments, David's dad appeared at the back door, the two men coming out behind him. Dad pointed up toward Copper Hill, making David and Linda duck self-consciously, completely out of sight. When David heard the screen door squeak shut, he peeked out again.

The two men were coming up the path. The one in the lead held the detector out before him, sweeping it over the ground as they walked up the path.

David tapped Linda's arm and jerked his head to the right; they moved silently from the tree to a patch of brush farther from the trail. Well hidden, they watched the men come over the crest of the hill, moving the detector in an arc from one side of the path to the other. They went down the other side and hopped off the short bank onto the sand.

The sand pit was big, about fifty yards across, and if they were going to search the whole thing, David knew they would be there for a while.

"What do you think they're looking for?" Linda asked.

"Something Dad told them about, I guess. But what?"

The men stayed close together, their eyes on the detector's gauges. Apparently something registered, because they huddled close to the device, one man pointing to a gauge. Excited now, they fanned out on the sand, their backs to one another as they searched. One of them called out over his shoulder, the other nodded.

Realization suddenly struck David hard. These men were not looking for them; he and Linda had no reason to hide from them. The two NASA men were walking into a trap! Dad had given them some story, told them something he knew would interest them enough to get them out on the sand, which was exactly where he wanted them because—

With no warning, the sand beneath the man with the detector began to whirl, creating a vortex that first spun him around, then began to suck him in. He dropped the detector and threw his arms up, opened his mouth to scream, but only had time to gasp—it was a long, ragged gasp, terrified and final.

The other man turned swiftly; his partner and the detector were gone and the whirlpool of sand was traveling across the pit toward him, moving with the speed and ease of a tornado. The man began to run for the embankment, but the sand beneath his feet shifted and swirled, making him sway this way and that until he tripped and fell.

"Oh my God!" Linda shouted, standing.

His arms straight up as he was sucked into the sand, the man screamed like a child, struggling against whatever was pulling him down.

He was gone.

The sand leveled, smoothed, and became still. It looked as if it had never been disturbed.

David and Linda stared open-mouthed at the pit for a long, silent moment. Then Linda grabbed David's shoulder firmly and began pulling him back the way they had come.

"Let's get the hell out of here," she said tremulously.

"Where are we going?" David asked as they got into the car.

"To a phone," Linda said breathlessly, starting the engine. With her hands gripping the wheel hard, she turned to David. Tears sparkled in her eyes. "David, I'm sorry."

"For what?"

"For . . . not believing you. Something horrible *is*

happening. It may not be what you think, but something's wrong." She jerked the gearshift and drove over the bumpy ground toward the paved road.

"What are we going to—" David swallowed his words as Linda slammed on the brakes. The car lurched to a halt in a cloud of dust.

As if from nowhere, the W. C. Menzies Elementary School bus rumbled before them, speeding down the road with Mrs. McKeltch at the wheel, hunched forward, her eyes narrowed and her jaw set.

Time seemed to slow down for David as he watched the bus drive by in a kind of slow motion. Mrs. McKeltch did not see them; she kept her eyes on the road, her neck straight and stiff. The bus was full of students, their faces in profile in the windows, familiar and yet . . . David realized with a sickening feeling that they were not really his classmates, his friends, not anymore. Eyes forward, mouths closed, they sat rigidly in their seats; there was no activity, there were no smiles. Although he was in Linda's car, David knew that, inside, the filled bus was silent as a tomb. And then he spotted Doug.

"Doug!" David screamed, throwing himself forward in the seat, clutching the dashboard desperately. "Doug, no!"

His best friend sat stiffly by the window, his mouth a firm, straight line; he was not talking, he was not laughing.

They had Doug.

"Oh, Jesus," Linda groaned painfully as the bus disappeared.

David did not hear her. He was trying hard not to cry, trying to hold back the tears that came from knowing he was the only one left. Mrs. McKeltch had taken them all. That could only mean that she'd want him even more now.

"What are we going to do?" David whispered, his voice raspy.

"We're going to get help."

Linda waited a moment, giving the bus a chance to get well ahead of them, then she pulled onto the road, kicking up dirt behind her.

"Who're you gonna call?" David asked.

"The state police. They're probably the safest bet."

"But what if . . ." David took a deep breath and swallowed hard.

"I know what you're thinking, and that's a definite possibility. We'll just have to be careful and take our chances, won't we?"

He nodded silently, wiping his eyes. David felt a pain unlike anything he'd ever experienced. It wasn't like twisting an ankle in kick ball. It wasn't like falling off a bike and getting skinned up. It eclipsed the biting pain in his knee. This pain was deep; it came from the very center of him, churning around inside him like a volcano on the brink of eruption. Tears came, but as a reaction, not a release. This was a pain for which there was no balm, no pill, no cure.

"Doug," he began, a sob hitching in his throat. "Doug was my best friend."

Linda looked over at him and lifted her foot from the pedal slightly, making the speeding car slow a bit. She reached over and took his hand, holding it tightly in hers.

"I know, David," she said, her voice soothing. "But . . . as cold as it sounds . . . we can't think about that now. We have to do something so this won't happen to anyone else—whatever it is."

Needing desperately to be close to someone, David slid over in the seat and Linda put her arm around him. He pressed his face into her shoulder. She felt warm and soft and he let his tears flow freely, realizing suddenly that she might be all he had left in the world.

"I'm scared," he spoke into her shoulder.

"I know, David. So am I."

In town, Linda pulled into a Taco Bell parking lot, turned off the ignition, and grabbed her purse.

"You stay here," she said. "I'll be right over there at the pay phone. I won't be long." Opening the door, she started to get out, then stopped and turned back to him. "Duck down. Stay out of sight." She slammed the door and headed for the pay phone, fishing through her purse for change.

David watched her as she hurried across the parking lot. His tears were gone, but the pain was not. It ate away at him insistently, like a vulture tearing the flesh from a corpse.

It was warm inside the car and as he slinked down in the seat, he cranked the window down, letting in the gentle, cooling breeze. He considered turning on the radio, but thought better of it; he didn't want to attract any attention. He closed his eyes and leaned back his head, trying to relax, trying to calm his jagged nerves. It felt good, the warm sun on his face, his arms limp at his sides, his eyes closed, locking his mind in a soothing blackness speckled with spots of dark color. . . .

As if from a great distance, David heard something pull into the parking lot . . . a truck maybe.

It stopped, its engine idled.

Footsteps . . .

Silence for a while, with just the breeze, the sunlight, and the darkness in his head.

The warmth suddenly disappeared as someone stepped up to the door. Thinking Linda had come back, David opened his eyes as a hand shot through the open window and gripped his collar, jerking him against the door.

"You missed the field trip, David Gardiner!" Mrs. McKeltch hissed, her prunish lips wriggling around her yellow teeth, her eyes narrow pits, the sunlight shining through stray wisps of her hair.

Panic shot through David like a jolt of electricity and he pulled away from her grasp, momentarily surprised when he succeeded. He threw himself behind the wheel and fumbled with the door handle as Mrs. McKeltch's feet clumped heavily on the pavement. David got the door open as she stormed around the front of the car, her hands reaching out for him. He didn't bother to close the door, he just tried to run.

She grabbed his shoulders and lifted him off the ground; his legs kicked out before him as he struggled within her powerful arms.

"You get an F for the day," she grunted through clenched teeth, dragging him toward the bus.

David spotted Doug standing in the open door of the bus, one hand on the rail, the other at his side; he wore that same sickly expression David had seen on his own dad's face. For a moment, David became limp in Mrs. McKeltch's hold.

"C'mon, David," Doug said quietly, "stop fighting."

"*No!*" David snapped, kicking back with both feet, feeling his heels dig into Mrs. McKeltch's shins. She did not let go, but she loosened her grip just enough for David to wrench himself from her arms. He landed on his feet and started running.

"Stop!" Mrs. McKeltch commanded.

He ignored her, running frantically into an alley between the Taco Bell and a self-service laundry. Pain burned like fire through his leg and his injured knee seemed to turn into putty. He tumbled over the pavement, slamming into a dumpster and landing on his back just in time to open his eyes and see Mrs. McKeltch bearing down on him like a truck with a sinister, steely grin. . . .

Linda punched the number of the state police for the third time and once again heard the warped, piercing tone followed by a mechanical female voice: "We're sorry. All circuits are busy now. Please hang up and try your—"

Linda slammed the receiver down so hard, the pay phone made a faint ring.

"Shit!" she spat, closing her eyes and rubbing them hard with her thumb and forefinger. A headache was beginning to pound in her head, gently now, like a distant drumbeat, but she knew it would get worse.

When she lowered her eyelids, they became movie screens, replaying the image of that school bus roaring by, filled with children sitting oddly still, their faces rigid and almost lifeless, Mrs. McKeltch at the helm with fire in her eyes.

What had she done to the children? What was happening in Willowbrook? Linda assumed it had something to do with the military, having seen those two NASA men disappear into the sand—another frightening image that played over and over in her head. If that was the case, the possibilities were terrifying. But she prayed there was some kind of perfectly benign explanation to everything.

She couldn't think about it anymore. She grabbed the receiver and angrily hit the buttons with her thumb.

The tone again, then the voice: "We're sorry. All circuits are—"

"*Damn!*" She jerked the door open and stepped out of the narrow, confined booth and took a deep breath of fresh air.

Looking up at the Taco Bell sign, Linda considered getting a bite to eat. Maybe David was hungry. The poor kid's stomach was probably a disaster.

Heading for the car, she saw that David was keeping himself well hidden. The seats looked empty. Then she saw the school bus and stopped in her tracks. Its door was open. Children sat silently in their seats, eyes forward.

Mrs. McKeltch was nowhere in sight.

"Oh, Christ, *David!*" she called, breaking into a run, dreading what she might see. When she found the car empty, she could barely contain her scream.

David began to crawl sideways away from Mrs. McKeltch, face up, moving like a crab over the pavement. The skin of his palms and elbows burned with cuts and scrapes.

Mrs. McKeltch was getting closer, blanketing him with a long, broad shadow. Her lips pulled back over her stained teeth, reminding David, for a moment, of a snarling attack dog. Her thick legs got bigger as she neared, looking like trees rooted in her black shoes, her wrinkled brown stockings clinging to the trunks like bark.

At the last possible instant, David rolled over on his hands and knees and began running even before he was standing. He rounded the corner of a building, hearing her pounding feet behind him, gaining . . . gaining. . . .

Pedestrians looked at him with alarm and annoyance as he dodged them, racing toward the corner.

Where's Linda? his mind screamed. *Why isn't she helping me?*

David stole a glance over his shoulder to see how close Mrs. McKeltch was.

She was gone.

Suspicious, he slowed to a jog, then a fast walk, looking again to make sure he hadn't just missed her.

She's afraid to be seen chasing a kid, he thought with relief.

He pressed on, trying not to look suspicious, trying not to pant too loudly. His face began to feel hot; pain sliced through his knee as well as his hands and elbows. He tried to ignore the pain, though. He trained his eye on the corner up ahead—it was getting closer and closer—tried to concentrate on it hard and use it to bury the feeling of pebbles under his kneecap. He hoped to find Linda around that corner, pulling out of the Taco Bell parking lot.

Instead he found Doug.

David froze at the corner. Doug was walking toward him, but didn't see him yet. He was looking, though, searching the sidewalk, looking this way and that, his eyes squinting in the sun. David was suddenly struck with an unwanted memory, a memory that hurt worse than the pain in his knee. He thought of a game he and Doug played a lot last summer, before school started. Pretending they were secret agents, they would walk through town, through shopping centers, searching for foreign spies. They would scan the pedestrians and shoppers and make up stories about them, creating elaborate backgrounds for the ones who stood out, who looked unusual. This one was from Russia where he'd spent years preparing himself for life in America, learning how to speak perfectly, dress perfectly, learning how to blend in without suspicion, without detection. But the front had not been perfect enough because David and Doug had spotted him; they could see through the facade, and they knew he was the enemy. That one was from Germany and he was secretly working toward the rebirth of the Nazi party; he followed the commands of Hitler's brain, which had been kept alive since the war. But the boys knew what he was up to.

The game had been fun then, but now it had been corrupted, perverted. The game was real and Doug was the enemy. He spotted David. His fists clenched and he began taking broader and faster steps toward him.

Limping back around the corner, David returned the way he'd come, hoping to go back through the alley and find Linda still in the lot. When he ducked into the narrow passage between the buildings, he came face to face with Mrs. McKeltch.

She smiled her dirty smile and hurried toward him.

David backed out of the alley, turned to his right—Doug was still coming, advancing quickly, his jaw set, eyes shrouded by a frown—then to his left. A policeman was marching toward him, his neck rigid, sunlight glinting off his badge.

Fear pounded in David's head in sync with his pain. The only thing left was to run into the street.

David whirled around as Linda's white Mustang convertible lurched to a halt at the curb. She leaned across the seat and opened the passenger door, shouting, "Get in, David, *get in!*"

David leaped at the car and threw himself inside. Linda began pulling onto the road before David was able to turn around and close the door; he nearly fell out of the car as he reached for it.

He sprawled in the seat for several moments, gasping to catch his breath, a fine shimmer of perspiration covering his face and making his shirt cling to his neck.

"Did ya call the—the state police?" he asked, gulping air.

"The lines were all busy," Linda said, sounding angry, frustrated, and worried. She glanced rapidly at David several times. "Are you all right?"

He nodded jerkily, licking his lips.

"Okay," Linda said, as if she were forming a plan. "I think there's a place we can hide while we call the FBI. A place they won't think to check."

"The FBI? What about the—"

"Yes, the FBI. Whatever's happening is too big for the police. *Much* too big."

Mrs. McKeltch watched the car speed recklessly down the main street of town. The drivers of other cars honked their horns and made obscene hand gestures. She paid them no attention, however; her eyes were locked on the white Mustang, and they narrowed as the car drove farther away and screeched around a corner, sped down a side street, out of sight.

In seconds, she was flanked by the policeman and the boy.

"Lost him again," Mrs. McKeltch said. "Because of that . . . that *bitch.*" She pressed her lips together so tightly that she almost seemed to have no mouth. Her eyes were cold, silent accusations as she looked first at the officer, then at Doug. She pivoted and stalked down the alley. "Let's finish with the others first," she said as they followed her. "We'll get the boy and the nurse eventually."

The final light of day faded as Linda slipped her key into the lock of the school's front entrance. Trembling, she twitched her head back and forth like a bird, looking for shadows, listening for sounds.

"Hurry!" David whispered, shuffling his feet nervously over the cement.

Linda had purposely taken the long way to the school, winding around the less traveled routes to avoid being seen. As she drove, David had remained silent, looking out at the lengthening shadows.

Trying to recover, she'd thought, looking at him. *I'm afraid that's gonna take a while.*

Once inside, Linda closed the door carefully, not wanting to make any noise. But as they crept down the empty, cavernous corridors, she found that would be difficult. Their careful footsteps echoed like falling rocks in the stillness.

When they got to her office, she unlocked the door.

"No!" David croaked, grabbing her wrist as she reached for the light switch. "No lights."

"Yeah," she agreed. "You're right." The boy was

sharp, even under pressure. She felt her way to the desk and the phone, then brushed her fingers over the buttons, feeling out 411.

"We're sorry. All circuits are busy now. Please—"

"God damn it!" she barked, louder than she'd intended, hanging up the phone. "Even directory assistance is busy."

David gasped softly in the darkness; it was the sound of a terrifying realization.

"Heather's dad," he breathed. "He must be messing with the lines."

"Who?"

Before David could explain, the room was awash with white light. Headlights were sweeping the parking lot, shining through the window. Tires crunched to a stop outside.

Linda ducked and pulled David down with her, peering over the windowsill. "My God," she groaned, "the police!"

Chapter Ten

The headlights blacked out; doors opened, then slammed.

Muffled footsteps.

Voices.

David watched Chief Ward and Officer Kenney approach the building with their flashlights shining before them. He prayed that they didn't see Linda's car.

"We've gotta get out of here," David said.

"How?"

"The back entrance. By the gym. C'mon." He stood and took her hand.

In the hall they both walked on tiptoe, but their footsteps still echoed hollowly. Favoring his left leg, David still managed to stay a step or two ahead of Linda, who kept looking over her shoulder.

Behind them, they could hear the faint rattle of keys outside the front entrance . . . the turning of the lock . . . the opening of the door. . . .

Linda squeezed his hand, as if to say, *They're inside!*

The policemen's heels clacked on the hard floor as they came in and started down the hall. Any moment, they would round the corner and spot David and Linda hurrying away.

Ahead and to the right, David spotted a sign which he'd passed many times. In the darkness, it was only a haze of red and white, but he knew what it said: BASEMENT—NO ADMITTANCE.

"This way!" he breathed, pulling Linda toward the door. He opened it and ushered her in, then cast a glance down the hall. Circles of light swept back and forth over the floor. He went through the door and pulled it shut.

They hurried down the concrete stairway until they came to a large metal sliding door. Grabbing the handle, David heaved it open with effort and let Linda through. Sliding it closed behind him, he turned and looked into the shadowy basement.

Total darkness was held back by a flickering ruddy glow that seeped between the doors of the two furnaces below. Dust hovered in the stuffy air. A metal staircase led to the basement floor with two small landings between the top and bottom. To the right, a catwalk stretched along three of the walls, ending in a descending ramp.

The boilers rumbled hungrily; something small and quick skittered over the cement floor.

They went down a few steps and stood on the first landing, pausing to listen for the policemen. Nothing yet. When they took another step, something clattered loudly.

Linda's foot had kicked a length of copper pipe left

on the landing. It rolled a few inches, then teetered on the edge of the step. Linda took in a sharp breath as she watched the pipe roll. For a moment, they were both paralyzed. David lifted his foot to step on the pipe, to prevent the racket that he knew it would make on the metal stairs.

He was too late.

The clatter echoed through the darkness, seeming to go on forever.

"Damn!" Linda rasped as they hurried to the floor.

"Over here!" David pulled her into a corner to their right. They huddled on a dirty old army cot in the corner, listening anxiously for footsteps overhead.

From their hiding place, David looked around the hazy basement. It was cluttered with the stuff of school life. A cardboard castle that had been used in a school play leaned against the brick wall. A rusty basketball hoop with no net lay atop a stack of old warped textbooks. Draped over a half-dozen plastic dairy crates was a bright red banner left over from a science show.

There were buckets and mops and brooms and rags, sponges that had become brittle and brushes that had lost their bristles. Taped to the side of a rusty old metal locker was a dog-eared picture of a half-naked woman. Two huge, wide furnaces dominated the basement, positioned side by side like two mumbling Buddhas. In the farthest corner, coal was piled beneath a chute.

What seemed to stand out—what caught David's attention most—was the copper. There were a half-dozen barrels of copper tubing, pipes, rods. Copper . . . It plucked a string in David's memory, but not hard enough. It wasn't clear yet, but the copper was somehow significant. . . .

Everywhere there was dust. It stung and tickled in David's nostrils with each inhalation. He coughed a few times and pressed his palm over his mouth.

An eternity of waiting and wondering passed. Had the two men gone? Had they seen Linda's car? Were more arriving?

"Jesus Christ," Linda whispered. "This is what I get for moving to California."

Her voice was childlike and tremulous. Guilt twisted in David's belly; he felt responsible for getting her into this.

"It's okay, Linda," he assured her softly, wishing he could say more or do something to make her stop trembling beside him.

"It's not okay! It's . . . it's ridiculous!"

She sounded angry, accusing. Was she doubting him? How could she after all that had happened? David said, "But you saw—"

"I don't know *what* I saw anymore." Her whispered voice was harsh and bitter, but no sooner were the words out than her arm was on David's shoulders. "Oh, I'm sorry, David. I'm just . . . I'm sorry."

"It's okay, Linda." He patted her hand, knowing well how she felt. "It's okay to be afraid."

"I'm not afraid. I'm *petrified!*"

"Me, too."

They pressed close together, taking refuge in one another's warmth. Despite the stifling dust, David could smell Linda's cinnamony perfume. It was comforting and . . . somehow . . . strange, though it seemed, considering their situation, the spicy scent was somehow exciting and, for a moment, he found that it had captured his full attention.

Then the door at the top of the stairs opened.

Powerful beams of light shined down into the basement.

A voice: "It came from down here."

It was Chief Ward.

Their feet clanked on the metal catwalk, slowly and cautiously.

David and Linda shrank back against the brick wall; David suddenly felt chilled to the bone despite the warmth of the furnaces.

The footsteps silenced.

"You hear that?" Kenney asked.

"What?"

David listened, but heard nothing at first. Then he felt it. It was very faint, a sort of soft buzz, but it began to get stronger, a bit louder, until it was a low growl that David could feel vibrating through the cot. It was something big, something moving fast and getting closer.

"The boiler?" the chief asked.

Hurrying to the stairs, Kenney said, "I don't think so." He and Chief Ward came down to the basement floor with their guns drawn.

It got louder and stronger, the vibrations humming through David's skin and into his bones, through his skull. Linda clutched his arm, terrified. From the dark corner where they were hidden, David had a clear view of Chief Ward and Officer Kenney, their guns ready, flashlights slicing the dark.

"It's the police," the chief called.

The vibrations became a tremor. . . .

"You can come out," he said. "We're here to help."

In a pig's eye, David thought.

The brick walls began to quiver as Chief Ward shined the light on them suddenly, blinding David for a moment. The round man smiled and said, "Miss Magnuson. David Gardiner. We've been looking for you."

David realized the vibration wasn't coming from above or from outside, but from below—from deep beneath the basement floor.

"Chief," Kenney said.

"Yeah?" He had to speak up because the rumbling was getting louder.

Gotta be ready to run, David thought, squeezing Linda's hand. *Something's comin'!* He could almost feel the blood pounding through his veins.

Officer Kenney shined his light on the floor. A hairline crack was spreading over the concrete, getting longer and wider by the second.

The chief said, "Let's get—"

A huge, domed head, gleaming and copper colored, tore through the concrete, spinning with deadly speed and force. Three amber eyes burned in the darkness, surrounded by bulging veins and curved blades that tapered to knifelike points protruded from its neck as it whirred loudly, madly swirling the dust in the air. Sharp ridges spiraled down its body like a giant screw.

The policemen screamed as they were thrown brutally upward, their arms and legs flailing. The blades silenced their cries. Skin tore silently; bones splintered with thick, heavy sounds; blood and flesh slapped onto the brick walls.

As the beast continued to rise, the two furnaces groaned metallically, torn from their foundations, belching fire. Great cracks crawled snakelike over the concrete, then blossomed like flowers, separating with solid crunching sounds. The metal supports beneath the stairs and catwalk quaked, then clanged as they began to collapse.

David watched the stairs tremble, knowing they were the only way out. He got to his feet, pulling Linda with him. Her face was white as a sheet, her jaw slack as she gawked at the creature. They stood against the wall, their hair blown by the force of the spinning blades.

David winced at the odor that suddenly filled the basement. It was the damp, pungent smell from the spaceship. He remembered the spiraled tunnel and realized how the creatures had dug through the earth: this thing had done it for them.

It craned its head as it rose and stared down at them with its three amber eyes, going higher and higher, its thick veins pulsing.

"Get ready!" David shouted.

"What?"

When it was high enough, David pulled hard on Linda's arm. "Now!" he screamed. "Run, *run*, RUN!" Hopping over crumbling chunks of concrete, dodging the lifeless and gored body of Chief Ward, David shot toward the stairs, praying that Linda would keep up. He flew up the stairs; they swayed precariously under his weight. He heard Linda's feet clattering behind him. David clutched the rail desperately as the staircase lurched a few inches away from the wall, its supports groaning as they pulled away from the bricks.

Six steps from the door. . . .

The creature's mushroomlike head rose above the catwalk; the blades tore away the railing, flinging it across the basement and against the wall. The giant knives whirred between David and the door.

"*David!*" Linda shrieked.

They froze on the stairs, watching the bulbous eyes.

For the first time in his life, David prepared to die, readied himself to be chopped in two. . . .

The whirring slowed. The creature's long body eased its spiraling to a stop.

There was a moment of silence that seemed to stretch on forever as the three eyes glared at them, as the creature became still and silent. Then it began to turn again, but in the opposite direction, slowly, like a fan that has just been plugged in, the hum of its motion beginning to churn the air around them.

"Come on!" David shouted, taking advantage of the moment and scaling the remaining steps two at a time.

The creature began to sink down as it spun. . . .

David grabbed the door handle and flung the heavy door aside with more strength than he knew he had. He and Linda flew up the concrete steps to the hall door, their footsteps thundered down the empty hall toward the front entrance.

His lungs were burning by the time he got to the car. With each heartbeat, his body seemed to swell with simultaneous fear and relief.

"Get in, get *in!*" Linda croaked, her voice dry and hoarse.

David flopped into the car seat and slammed the door as Linda started the ignition and revved the car through the empty parking lot. They passed the Willowbrook Police car and roared onto the road.

"Thuh-thuh-they must be tun-tunneling under the whole *town!*" David gasped.

"What're we gonna do?"

"Stop 'em! We've gotta stop 'em!"

"*How?*" Linda shouted. "They're everywhere!

Let's just keep driving and get the hell out of this crazy town!"

"We can't just leave." David's voice softened. "We've gotta find my mom and dad. . . ."

Linda's panic began to fade slowly; she spoke with confidence and reason. "We're *not* going back there alone. We need help."

"Yeah," David agreed. But who? The only other people in the world he trusted—his parents—were no longer his parents. Unfallen tears burned in his head as he thought of his mother tickling him through the covers of his bed, growling like a bear . . . and of his dad getting excited about the brilliant meteorite in the night sky, laughing like another kid instead of like a—

Dad's laugh. The way he always laughed when he said "Mad Dog"?

Mad Dog Wilson.

David jerked around in the seat and faced Linda, his lower lip tucked confidently between his teeth. He took in a deep breath and let it out through the hopeful words, "General Wilson!"

Linda's mind was reeling. Her head was pounding and there was a shrill ringing in her ears. Suddenly nothing seemed safe. After what she had seen, her very own car seemed a possible threat. Having witnessed something that, earlier, woud have seemed impossible, the word "impossible" lost all meaning and she dared not even guess what might happen next.

It had obviously been a living thing that had come up through the basement floor, but there had been something very machinelike about it. The bone-rattling whir of the blades . . . the amber eyes shining like headlights. . . .

When she thought of how close she and David had come to meeting the same fate as the two policemen, Linda felt like vomiting.

"They killed two of their own people," David said thoughtfully, fidgeting on the edge of the seat like a housefly, never holding still for a second. "As if they didn't matter."

"Maybe they didn't," Linda suggested.

David frowned and sucked his lips between his teeth. "It must have been after something, that thing. There was no reason to tunnel into the basement. Except . . . the copper . . ."

"What?"

"Didn't you see all the copper in the basement? There were barrels of it." He became distant and withdrawn.

"Well? What about the copper?"

He shook his head. "I don't know. Just an idea. My pennies were stolen. And the smell in the ship . . ." He turned away from her and looked out the window. When he said no more, she didn't press him.

Linda had passed Camp Puller several times. During the day, it appeared very official, a sterile and bustling complex. At night, however, it seemed forbidding. The chain-link fence seemed taller; the curved posts strung with barbed wire at the top seemed to frown discouragingly at anyone who might consider entering. Beyond the fence, well off the road, the base glowed with activity.

The needle was approaching seventy on the speedometer as Linda drove along the fence and she lifted her foot from the pedal, unaware that she'd been speeding. The tires screeched lightly over the pavement as she swerved onto the narrow road leading to the base.

The headlights fell on the guard station where two MPs, looking nervous and stiff, stepped to the center of the road and waved their arms for Linda to slow down. She braked and eased to a stop, rolling down her window. One of the young men came to the door and leaned his head through the opening. His neck was thick, his face hard and without expression.

"What's going on here, ma'am?" he asked sternly.

"We have to see General Wilson!" David insisted, his voice ragged.

"It's urgent," Linda added, hoping David wouldn't say anything that sounded crazy. *"Please!"*

"Do you have clearance?" the MP asked.

"My dad, George Gardiner, works here!" David shouted. "Except he's . . . he's not my dad any—"

"David, please." Linda tried to sound urgent, but calm. "I'm the nurse from Menzies Elementary School. There's a serious health problem in town. You *must* call General Wilson."

"I'm sorry, ma'am."

David threw himself toward Linda, toward the open window. "A spaceship landed behind my house!" he cried. "They got my mom and dad, the Willowbrook Police . . . the whole town! We tried to call the FBI!"

Linda squeezed his shoulder and tried to quiet him. "David, let me." She turned to his rock-hard face.

"Ma'am," he said, "I'm going to have to ask you to leave the premises. Now."

"No, no, listen. I know it sounds crazy. It sounded crazy to me, too. But a few minutes ago, I was almost killed. There are . . . well, *creatures* here. From . . .

well they're not from this earth, that's for sure. And they're spreading. Taking over the whole area."

One corner of his mouth twitched into a smirk as he put a hand on the edge of the door. "Ma'am . . ."

"Please, just call General Wilson for us. Tell him what we've said." As a last resort, she placed her hand on the MP's and gave him her softest, most pleading look. "Please?"

General Wilson's office was dark but for the glow coming from a bank of video monitors against one wall. The monitors displayed various angles of a rocket on a launching pad. Spotlights washed over the rocket as a countdown appeared in the top right corner of each screen. There was no volume; the office was silent.

General Wilson was seated before the monitors in a swivel chair, his thumb and forefinger tugging at his rock-hard jaw, craggy frown lines spanning his forehead. His cheekbones were looking sharper than usual with dark hollows below them. General Wilson had been losing weight lately. He always lost weight when he worried, and he'd been worrying a lot lately about the Millennium Project.

It was important and it had to go smoothly. Until the rocket was well on its way, General Wilson would wonder if something had been overlooked, if the smallest of details had slipped by unchecked. He had the utmost faith in the men and women who had worked so long and hard on the project, but there had already been a number of mishaps, and nobody was perfect.

That someone had failed at his or her job was not all that concerned General Wilson. He was by nature a worrier, but his imagination was working overtime these days. What if someone had leaked information about the top-secret project? Whether accidentally or intentionally—perhaps even for money—a leak could damage security and might increase the chances of sabotage. And if there were a major complication—an explosion or something—there would be publicity, which could taint the base's otherwise spotless reputation.

General Wilson hoped that what *could* happen and what *would* happen would be two different things and that everything would move along without a hitch. But like rats within walls, his worries skittered and nibbled. . . .

Captain Rinaldi stood at his side, leaning forward on the back of an empty chair, also watching the monitors.

Their faces glowed with bluish light in the silence.

Both men started when the phone rang.

"Base commander's office, Captain Rinaldi."

General Wilson turned to him, cocked a brow, and prepared himself for the worst, as always.

"Yes . . . who?" Rinaldi held the receiver to General Wilson. "Provost marshall's office, sir."

General Wilson stood and cleared his throat heartily. "Yes? . . . What? *Invaded?* Sounds like another crazy. Well, just—hm? . . . Gardiner's boy, huh? Well . . . it just might affect security. Send them up. . . . No, *no,*" he said sharply, "have them *driven.*" He hung up and turned to Rinaldi, frowning. "I hope I'm wrong," he said softly. "I have been before. But something in my gut tells me that we've got trouble."

The base was a nest of activity. Floodlights brightened some areas, while others were dim and alive with shadows. Everywhere there was movement; jeeps whizzed around with important-looking men in the back seats and Marines hurried this way and that, carrying boxes, calling out to one another. At every turn, there were sentries standing tall, straight and watchful.

After Linda's Mustang was parked, an MP had escorted her and David to a Jeep. They got in the back seat and the quiet, stern man drove them across the base.

From the Jeep, David tried to take in everything around him. He'd never seen so much activity at the base. Something was happening, something important and, most likely, secret, since his dad had said nothing about it to him.

The MP drove the Jeep into a smaller compound enclosed by barbed wire. There were uniformed men rushing in every direction.

Steam billowed all around, giving shadows lives of their own, adding mystery to the compound as men disappeared and reappeared, passing in and out of the mist like ghosts.

David spotted several men bustling around a large liquid-oxygen fuel truck. David gasped and clutched Linda's arm, blinking several times to make sure his eyes weren't failing him.

Carrying a huge crate to the truck were the two technicians who had been sucked into the sand pit earlier.

"Look!" David whispered, pointing vaguely. "It's those two guys. . . ."

Behind them, two other technicians were loading spindles of copper wire into a NASA pickup truck.

"More copper," David said.

Leaning toward his ear, Linda whispered in a quavering voice, "I don't like this."

As the Jeep drove on, a black Bronco crossed its path at the rear, slowing to a stop. George Gardiner got out and slammed the door. He wore NASA coveralls and carried a metal case. With cautious glances in every direction, he approached the two technicians he had lured to the sand pit that day. Nodding, he said, "Hollis. Johnson."

They nodded in return, unsmiling.

"It's wired," he said confidently.

Taking the case, Hollis said, "Good. Then everything's set."

Gardiner turned and hurried back to the Bronco. Before starting the ignition, he turned to a blank-faced Ellen Gardiner, sitting motionless in the passenger seat, and said quietly, "It's just a matter of time now."

To David Gardiner, General Wilson had always been a bit of a joke. The man's discomfort in the classroom and the nickname that David's dad had given him had lent him a sort of fumbling air.

Now, seated at his big desk, his face dark, he almost seemed a different man entirely. On the wall behind him hung pictures of General Wilson and Richard Nixon, Henry Kissinger, and Ronald Reagan, all personally signed. In each picture, General Wilson's face glowed with pride. All around the pictures, weapons were mounted on the wall: rifles, handguns, knives.

The man behind the desk was no longer just the deep-chested general who spoke in class once every year. He was no longer "Mad Dog" Wilson. He was David's last chance.

Asking to see the back of the man's neck before saying anything had been a nearly unbearable but necessary embarrassment to David.

"The back of my *neck?*" General Wilson had replied with a squint, glancing at Captain Rinaldi.

Linda had spoken up for David. "He's serious, General," she'd said. "Please."

David had almost cried out with relief when he found nothing on the general's neck. He'd seated himself before the desk beside Linda and, covering every detail, he'd told his story.

When he was finished, the general locked his big hands together on the desktop and leaned forward, frowning.

"That's one hell of a story, David," he said. "And honestly, I've heard quite a few in the Marine Corps."

"I know it must sound utterly ridiculous, General," Linda said. "But I can assure you that every word of it is true."

Turning to Captain Rinaldi, the general said, "Get on the phone and check out that sighting."

Rinaldi immediately picked up the phone and spoke in quiet tones.

"I don't know," General Wilson said to David. "People getting sucked under the sand . . . aliens running loose under the town. It's all just a little hard to swallow."

David's head buzzed. Trying to sound convincing, he said, "But if it *is* true and you don't do anything—at least look *into* it—something horrible's gonna happen!"

The general rubbed his chin for a while, searching David's face.

"Sir," Rinaldi said, hanging up the phone, "NASA

confirms a visual sighting during the meteor shower two nights ago. But radar reported no strike."

David shot to his feet and leaned on General Wilson's desk. "But what if their ship absorbed energy?" he asked frantically. "What if it could hang onto those energy bursts? It wouldn't show up on your radar because no energy would bounce back!"

"You're a very bright boy, David, but . . ."

"Sir," Rinaldi said, "a search team was sent out to look for a sign of impact or landing. The two men who checked out the Copper Hill area gave a clean report."

David spread his arms and gestured with exasperation. "That's because they were sucked under the sand! They're part of it now! General, whatever's supposed to happen is gonna happen at midnight."

General Wilson and Captain Rinaldi exchanged a forboding glance.

"Midnight," the general said quietly with dread. He turned to Linda and smiled vaguely. "Ma'am, could you and the boy leave us for a moment?" To Rinaldi, he said, "Take them next door. Tell NASA that I'm doing a routine security check on their men. I don't want to make an issue of this, but I want to speak with the two men who checked out Copper Hill."

"Yes, sir."

Before being ushered out of the office, David looked up at General Wilson and asked quietly, "Do you believe me?"

"I'm going to see what's going on, David," the general said, patting David's back. "Don't worry. Everything will be fine."

But General Wilson knew that everything was not fine. Midnight was the time set for the launching of the rocket. Something was afoot, and it didn't look good.

Rinaldi stuck his head in the office. "Shall I have Curtis send them in when they arrive, sir?"

General Wilson motioned for him to come in and close the door. "I want you to stand over there, behind the door. Just in case they try anything."

"Do you expect them to, sir?"

"I don't expect anything, but I want to be ready for everything."

Rinaldi stood beside the closed door and they waited.

When Hollis and Johnson entered, they looked grim and stiff, as if tense about seeing the general. They stepped before the desk and waited for him to speak. The general was careful not to glance at Rinaldi.

"Gentlemen," General Wilson said, "I have a few ques—"

The two men instantly pulled guns.

Rinaldi dove from his spot behind the door and threw an arm around each man's neck, pulling them over backwards. Johnson's gun went off harmlessly.

"Curtis!" General Wilson barked.

Two MPs rushed into the office with guns drawn and held on Hollis and Johnson; Curtis was right behind them.

"You're under arrest!" Rinaldi growled, getting to his feet.

The men on the floor let their guns slide from their hands as they watched the general round his desk and stand over them.

"Now," General Wilson said with quiet threat, "you two are going to tell me just what the *hell* this is all about."

Handcuffs clinked as the MPs unlatched them from their belts.

"Well—" General Wilson folded his arms over his chest. "—I'm waiting."

Johnson's mouth was open, he was about to speak, when he and Hollis suddenly arched their backs. They became rigid on the floor, their mouths stretched open, their eyes bulbous. Making straining, gurgling sounds in their throats, Hollis and Johnson simultaneously slapped their hands to the backs of their necks, writhing in silent agony.

The others watched the spasms in horror. General Wilson's arms dropped to his sides and he gasped, "Jesus, what's—"

Hollis and Johnson relaxed; their eyes rolled into their heads, shining like white marbles. In an instant, they became very still.

Rinaldi dropped to his knees and touched their throats, feeling for a pulse. Slowly, he pulled his hand away and looked up at the general. "They're dead."

"Christ," General Wilson sighed.

The dead men still held their necks, as if their pain had not gone away. Rinaldi turned Johnson over and moved his hand aside.

"What's that?" General Wilson asked, leaning forward to get a look at a cut on the back of the man's neck.

"I don't—"

Before Rinaldi could touch it, something began to ooze from the small incision, something long and thin. It rotated as it slid out of Johnson's neck.

"Shit!" the general snapped.

The needle was very delicate, copper-colored, with

tiny hieroglyphics engraved on the side. It spun its way out of the man's neck and rolled onto the floor, glistening with fluids. Another one rolled out from under Hollis's neck.

"Don't touch it!" General Wilson said, stepping back. "What . . . ever it is."

As the needles rolled to the center of the floor, Rinaldi quickly got to his feet and stepped out of their way.

Curtis, the MPs, Rinaldi, and General Wilson watched the needles in amazement.

They glistened with blood and a strange luminescent green fluid, reflecting slivers of light. Tendrils of smoke rose from the needles as they began to sizzle.

As if sensing something dangerous were about to happen, all the men took a step back.

With a sharp *pop*, the needles exploded, sending up puffs of greenish smoke.

A second later, General Wilson ordered, "Seal the base perimeter! Alert security! And get those NASA boys down here *immediately!* I want the kid and the nurse brought back here *now!*"

With hurried "Yes, sirs," Curtis and the MPs rushed from the room and Rinaldi grabbed the phone.

General Wilson stepped in the doorway and called after the men, "And lock up the launch, for God's sake!"

Chapter Eleven

After returning to General Wilson's office, David stared in amazement at the bank of video monitors. Below the rocket on the launching pad were incomprehensible readouts, data that he someday hoped to understand.

Linda stood beside him, distant and preoccupied.

Taking his attention from the monitors, David listened to the conversation going on across the room. Voices were being raised impatiently. General Wilson was talking with two men. One, a young man with short-cropped dark hair, wore a white coat and looked frustrated, a bit angry. The other was older, with tired eyes below receding, frizzy gray hair. He wore a gold corduroy sport coat, a plaid shirt, and brown tie. He seemed weary.

"No!" the young man snapped adamantly, his arms stiffening at his sides. "Any further delays and we'll miss the launch window!"

The old man held something long and thin between his fingers, jagged and black as coal. Inspecting it carefully, he said, "Mars won't wait for us, General."

"I understand, gentlemen," the general said placatingly. "We will go tonight, I assure you. But we have to be able to guarantee security first." He took the small black object from the old man and held it up before his face, squinting at it, his lips parted. "We still don't know what the hell we're dealing with here."

Impatiently, the young man asked, "What do you suggest?"

"I want to put a temp freeze on countdown," General Wilson said, "until we're all clear. Then it's your show."

The old man put a hand on General Wilson's shoulder. "You got yourself a deal."

"What's it going to Mars for?" David asked, walking toward them.

The men looked at one another for a moment, then turned to David.

"Is it a manned mission?" David went on when he got no reply.

The general was reluctant. "Well it's . . . it's not manned, David. But it *is* a soft landing."

"But why?"

"We're looking for life," the old man said simply.

David's eyes widened.

"Er, uh, Doctor," the general said, "this is the Gardiner boy. David, this is Dr. Stout, senior scientist on the Millennium Project, and—" He gestured to the younger man. "—this is Dr. Weinstein of S.E.T.I."

Stout smiled and shook David's hand. "How do you do, David."

Weinstein nodded, but did not smile.

"S.E.T.I.," David muttered, looking at the young doctor. "That's Search for Extraterrestrial Intelligence. So . . . you expect to find life on Mars." He turned to Dr. Stout. "I didn't think the Viking Missions found any sign of life. Except . . ." Something in David's memory was jarred. He thought quickly to get a handle on it. Something he'd read . . . a picture he'd seen. "I remember! I saw this picture in a magazine. It showed these things on the surface, like . . . they looked like pyramids."

"I saw that, too," Linda said, breaking her long, nervous silence.

"Yeah," David went on, "and what about that gigantic thing that looked like . . . wasn't it a monkey's head? It was in all the papers. It was a fake, right?"

Glancing at General Wilson, Dr. Stout slipped his hands into his coat pockets and said, "On the contrary. There were other photos too . . . too sensational to be made public."

David scratched his head. Something wasn't right; something about all this didn't fit. When it finally struck him, he spread his arms in confusion. "But what about *water?* There's not enough water on Mars to support life!"

"On the *surface,*" the old man said, running fingers through his wiry white hair. "That's why we're looking below ground this time. Recent data from Viking suggests the possibility of subterranean life."

David's eyes locked with Linda's; they were both thinking the same thing, David was sure.

"The tunnels . . ." Linda whispered.

"And if there *is* something up there," General

Wilson added gravely, "it might not want to be found."

The thoughtful atmosphere in the room was shattered by Curtis's sharp, urgent voice. *"Look!"* He pointed to the monitors and everyone huddled around them.

Men were scurrying everywhere about the rocket, waving their arms, pointing guns. Some were running from, others running after, a fuel truck that was speeding toward the launch pad. Plastic containers were attached to the truck's sides, jostling as it sped a path through the men.

"Those are explosives!" the general bellowed, leaning toward the monitors.

"Oh, God, the rocket," the old man mumbled with quiet dread.

Klaxons began to sound, and just as suddenly silenced. The lights darkened, the monitors blanked, and the office was filled with an instant of forbidding silence.

The general shouted, "Everybody get—"

Too late.

With a rush of skull-splitting sound, the windows of the office shattered inward. Linda screamed as everyone sprawled on the floor.

MPs rushed into the office with flashlights; one of them shouted, "Is anybody hurt?"

In a second, the general was back on his feet, ignoring the question, yelling, "Go to auxiliary base power, *now!*"

Rinaldi scrambled to his feet, crunched over broken glass to the phone, and tried to dial.

"General," he said frantically, "the outside lines are down."

"God damn it!" the general roared, pounding a fist on the desktop. He turned to one of the MPs. "Get us back on line!"

"I'll see what I can do, sir." He rushed out, calling to someone beyond the open door.

David got on his knees and held his hands before him. It was dark, but he saw no cuts on his palms. He touched his face and ran a hand through his hair. Turning to Linda, he said, "Are you all right?"

"Yes," she said, sniffling. "Just scared. What . . . happened?"

"Somebody blew up the Millennium," Dr. Stout said wearily.

"It's *them!*" David shouted. "They don't want you up there! That's why they came here, to Willowbrook! To destroy the Millennium."

The lights flickered several times, then came on. A raging fire appeared on the monitors.

Staring at one of the screens, Dr. Stout shook his head slowly and said, "It's gone. Completely wiped out."

All eyes turned to the monitors as a smaller secondary explosion erupted into the sky.

The phone rang and Rinaldi snatched it up.

"Sir," he said to the general after listening for a moment, "operations reports that radar was momentarily down, but it's back in service now."

"Anything coming in?" General Wilson asked anxiously.

"Negative, sir."

The general nodded knowingly. "They're already here." He turned to David and bent down, bracing his hands on his thighs. "David, can you take us to that place? That sand pit?"

"Yeah. It's right behind my house."

Standing, he began snapping orders. "Rinaldi, get a transport officer on the phone and find out if alert force is standing by. Curtis, take a platoon and head for the school."

"Yes, sir!"

Putting a big hand on David's head, General Wilson said confidently, "Don't worry, David. The United States Marine Corps has no qualms about killing martians."

Numbed by all the excitement, the pain in David's knee had become no more than a dull ache. He sat in the back seat of another Jeep with Linda. General Wilson was in front and Captain Rinaldi was driving.

Two light assault vehicles led the way to the sand pit. Each one was crammed with armed troops and mounted with 25mm chain guns. There were even more behind them, some armed with TOW antitank missiles, all carrying more troops, a rumbling parade of green metal and canvas.

General Wilson turned to David and Linda, handing each of them a pouch. "These attach to your sides," he said. "Inside are gas masks. Just in case."

"Wow!" David gasped, opening his pouch.

"Hang on, David, hang on," General Wilson chuckled. "That's just in case."

"Oh." David snapped the pouch shut, nodding. "Okay." He turned to Linda; she was expressionless, eyes forward. She seemed lost in thought, oblivious to the activity around her. Touching her hand lightly, he said, "Are you okay?"

She turned to him suddenly, as if awakened from a doze. "Yeah," she said breathlessly. "I'm okay. Just a little—" A smile flicked over her lips. "—overwhelmed."

General Wilson suddenly bellowed, "What the hell is that?"

David gripped the seat before him and pulled himself forward. Ahead of them, a police car had been parked lengthwise across the street, blocking their path. Others were on the shoulder. Policemen gathered on each side of the street while a single officer strode to the middle of the street. He held a shotgun.

The two assault vehicles ahead of the Jeep separated so Rinaldi could drive between them. As they neared the roadblock, David recognized the policeman standing in the street.

"He chased me in the street today!" David shouted, pointing. "He's one of them, General!"

As the Jeep rolled to a stop, General Wilson stood.

The officer held up a hand and shouted, "Stop! This is the police! No one is allowed through!"

The general leaned toward Captain Rinaldi and said quietly, "Pull over."

As Rinaldi backed up the Jeep and drove to the shoulder, General Wilson motioned for a third assault vehicle to come forward. It was armed with antitank missiles.

"*This,*" General Wilson shouted, "is the Marines! We're on official government business! If you don't clear the road, we *will!*" He turned to the drivers of the vehicles beside him and nodded, putting on his gas mask. Everyone, including David and Linda, followed suit.

The policeman raised his shotgun and aimed at the general, but tear-gas cannisters were exploding before he could pull the trigger. White gas billowed over the road, engulfing the police cars and officers. The men staggered and coughed, clutching their throats.

Waving an arm, General Wilson commanded, "Get that goddamned heap out of the way!"

One of the Marines on the middle assault vehicle nodded and fired the cannon mounted before him.

The police car erupted into a ball of fire and blew out of the road like a leaf in a breeze, mowing down several of the wretching policemen.

General Wilson patted Rinaldi's shoulder and said, "Take off."

As they drove through the swirling wall of gas, David could see the policemen kneeling and lying on the road, hacking and writhing. Those who had been struck by the flaming car were sprawled motionless, some with small spots of flames burning on their uniforms.

Linda put a hand to her forehead, clenched her eyes, and turned away.

As the convoy was speeding toward the sand pit, Curtis and his men were blowing their way through the locked doors of W. C. Menzies Elementary School. The man firing his automatic weapon stopped, stepped forward, and kicked aside the jagged glass and remaining shards of wood, clearing a path for the others.

The puttering of two helicopters descending outside was muffled by the heavy footfalls of the men as they hurried down the dark hall with Curtis and Dr. Weinstein in the lead.

His pistol drawn, Curtis shined his high-powered flashlight on every door they passed.

"The boy said it was in the basement," Weinstein said.

"I know that," Curtis snapped. He resented the doctor's presence, certain he would only get in the way. His light passed over the red and white sign. "This is it," he said, pushing the door open.

At the foot of the first staircase, Curtis slid the metal door aside and the troops thundered down the metal stairs into the basement, coming to a sudden halt halfway down.

The furnaces were mangled around the edges. The staircase hung unsteadily from its supports. Chunks of concrete were scattered over what was left of the floor. In the center of it all was a hole, perhaps twelve feet in circumference, from which an orange glow illuminated the dark basement.

From the landing, Curtis could tell that the hole was very deep, and whatever had made it had been big. Shaking his head with slowly growing disbelief, he muttered, "Jesus H. Christ."

Troops swarmed around David's house. They charged up the walk ahead of him, nearly knocking him over. When they found the door to be locked, they broke it down.

David watched with alarm as they plowed into the house. He stopped on the path and watched as more of them stormed through the broken front door. Through the darkened windows, he could see the darting beams of their flashlights.

Didn't they realize that someone *lived* there? Couldn't they be a little more careful?

A helicopter hovered over the house, its spotlight shining like a bar of daylight over the house and yard.

David hurried into the house, ignoring Linda's call.

"David! David, wait!"

Inside, the men were rushing up the stairs, going through the rooms and closets one by one.

"Hey!" David shouted when a blue vase of silk flowers was knocked to the floor. The vase shattered and the pieces crunched under stomping feet.

David raced up the stairs to his room, trying light switches along the way. The power was out. From the open doorway of his bedroom, David watched as the troops walked over his toys. Godzilla's head was crushed, the cardboard Tokyo was flattened, a plastic robot was shattered, comic books and magazines were torn underfoot.

"This is my *room!*" David cried.

He was ignored. The men opened his closet and looked under the bed.

"David," Linda said behind him. "Let's go outside. We might be in the way here."

"But . . . my *things* . . ."

He let her lead him down the hall, down the stairs.

They don't care, he thought. *The house doesn't matter to them. They just want to find the martians.*

They went out the back door and stood in the yard. Lights were shining beyond Copper Hill; voices called and the hulking assault vehicles rumbled. Linda took David's hand and started up the path.

Tension ached in David's neck and shoulders and his eyes stung with tears. This wasn't what he'd wanted when he turned to General Wilson for help. True, the martians had to be stopped. But most important of all to David were his parents—he wanted them back. They were somewhere within the bowels of the ship, most likely. And if they weren't, David knew that was where he could break the link that held them to the martians.

At the crest of the hill, they saw winches being set up. Vehicles were surrounding the pit. Bright floodlights washed over the sand making it gleam a pure white.

Linda gasped when the squad leader, a short, bullet-shaped man, charged past them and went over the hill toward the general. They followed him, picking up their pace.

"General," the squad leader said, "the house is all clean, sir."

"Fine, thanks," General Wilson said. He was frowning, preoccupied. He'd been talking to a tall black lieutenant when the squad leader approached.

David stepped forward to get the general's attention. "General Wilson."

Distracted, the general glanced down at him. "Yes, David?"

"General, what about my *parents?* Are we going to find them?"

"Well, David—"

"General," the lieutenant interrupted, "about those winches . . ."

"Uh, yes, um—" To David, he said, "We're doing our best, David, I promise you." Turning his back to the boy, he followed the lieutenant. "Okay, Lieutenant Bryce, let's have a look."

David trailed after him.

"David," Linda said, following, "will you stay in one place!"

At the edge of the sand pit, David and Linda watched as Lieutenant Bryce waved four Jeeps into position with winches and thick, heavy cables. Captain Rinaldi walked along the perimeter of the sand pit shouting orders.

David spotted several of the men standing on the sand cutting away brush at the edge to clear a field of fire. He pointed at them and tugged on Linda's arm. "Look! They're on the sand!"

Rinaldi saw them, too, and broke into a run. "Hey! Get outta there!" Flailing his arms, he herded them off the sand, stepping for just a moment—a very brief moment—off the embankment and into the pit.

It happened in a heartbeat. The sand spun beneath him, twirling him around like a nightmarish music-box dancer. Before he could make a sound, he was gone.

"General!" David screamed, running toward him. He pointed toward the sand pit.

"Rinaldi!" the general shouted, his jaw slack. "Holy Christ! Get away from there!" he ordered the other men around the pit. He turned to the lieutenant. "Get those damned winches ready!" Standing next to him, David heard the general mumble under his breath, "We're gonna blow those bastards off the map."

Curtis and his men had climbed down the hole, using the spiraled ridges as rungs. At the bottom, the hole intersected with a tunnel. With flashlight beams dancing on the curved walls, they proceeded cautiously. It was not terribly dark; light came from somewhere, but it was a strange light, a warm amber color.

Several yards ahead, the tunnel curved. Knowing that at any moment something could appear around the bend, Curtis pressed on slowly.

There was an instant of blinding light, there and gone in a flash, from beyond the curve.

"Hit the floor!" Curtis shouted.

The men dropped, their weapons ready.

Silence . . .

Then, approaching quickly from around the bend, footsteps . . .

Heavy and clumsy . . .

"Let's see what we've got here," Curtis whispered, aiming his pistol, readying himself for a fight.

Shadows appeared on the wall of the tunnel, enormous, hulking shadows bobbing over the ridges.

Curtis's voice was hoarse when he muttered, "Son . . . of a . . . *bitch!*"

There were three of them and they were huge; folds of lizardlike skin drooped over their fat faces and around their enormous jaws. They sloshed as they hobbled down the tunnel toward them, stopping when they spotted the men. One of the creatures grunted.

Dr. Weinstein jumped to his feet and raised a hand. "Hold your fire!" he shouted at the men.

"Get *down,* God damn it!" Curtis growled.

Weinstein turned to Curtis and said pleadingly, "We can't just blow away an opportunity like this. *Look* at these things! We don't know what they hell they are!"

"Exactly . . ."

One of the creatures held an oval-shaped pod in its pincered hand and raised it a few inches from its side as all three of them stepped back pensively.

"Wait," Weinstein whispered, approaching them cautiously. He smiled. "Take it easy. . . ." Reaching into his coat, he removed the charred remains of one of the copper needles that had come from the necks of Hollis and Johnson. "This is yours . . . right? It *is* yours, isn't it?"

The creature holding the pod stepped forward.

Dr. Weinstein stiffened nervously but held his

ground. "That's it," he said. "I am Dr. Weinstein. Yes . . ." He beckoned the creature forward. "Come on . . ."

It took another step, its nostrils flaring as it sniffed wetly at the doctor's hand. It looked into Weinstein's eyes, blinking several times, a curious expression wrinkling its huge brow.

"I'm a scientist," the doctor went on. "I'm from the Search . . . for Extraterrestrial . . . Intelligence. Do you understand me? I won't hurt you. We just want to . . . *understand* you."

With a moist, tearing sound, a seam split in the pod and it opened like an eye.

Weinstein froze, staring at it curiously.

A sliver-thin beam shot from the pod and the young doctor screamed in agony—a shrill, ragged scream that sounded as if it might tear out his throat—then burst into flames. In an instant, he was gone, leaving behind a few wisps of smoke.

Before Curtis could give the order, the men opened fire, blowing large chunks of the creatures onto the walls of the tunnel. Arms were torn from the beasts, fat eyes popped, long, glistening fangs chipped and shattered, and gaping wounds gushed a thick green fluid over the ground. The troops continued firing and the creatures sprayed through the tunnel like confetti.

When the echoes of the gunfire died down, Curtis stood and grimaced at the oozing remains scattered about them. Taking a deep, steadying breath, he waved for the men to follow him deeper into the long, twisting tunnel.

David felt as if he might explode. They were going to blow up the sand pit. They were trying to destroy the ship! He saw them preparing bricks of explosives and winches to pull the men to safety if the vortex should open up again. His breathing was fast; he was beginning to feel dizzy and panicky.

What if Mom and Dad are down there? a voice in his head screamed.

Linda put an arm around him, as if sensing his fear, and said, "They're doing all they can, David."

The general was giving more orders. Men were scurrying everywhere like ants. Engines rumbled and exhaust fumes dirtied the air. They were going to kill the martians . . . and perhaps kill his parents with them.

David broke away from Linda and dashed for the sand pit, his heart in his throat.

"David, *nooo!*" Linda screamed.

"Hey, kid!" one of the Marines shouted. "Come back here! You *crazy?*"

"David, please!"

He looked over his shoulder and saw Linda following him. He wanted her to stay—he wanted to do this alone!

"I have to find my mom and dad!" he called to her, hoping she'd stay. But she kept coming.

"Come back here *now!*" she snapped angrily.

"Hey, lady!" another Marine barked.

Others began shouting, telling them to turn back, to stay away from the sand.

David dove off the embankment, landed on his feet, then fell flat on his face. He scrambled up again and began running to the center of the pit.

"David, please *stop!*" Linda pleaded, closer now.

He glanced back to see her running over the sand beside him, gaining rapidly.

Linda threw herself on him and they both tumbled to the sand. She grabbed his arm and jerked him to his feet. He could hear her gasping with fright as she began dragging him back to the embankment.

They were only a few feet from the edge of the pit when the sand beneath them began to collapse, then swirl, pulling them down. David heard more shouts from the men and from General Wilson. He heard Linda scream as they were pulled into the pit.

In a moment, he heard nothing at all. . . .

Chapter Twelve

The men around the pit froze and stared silently at the motionless sand. Several of them turned toward General Wilson.

"Sir," Lieutenant Bryce said breathlessly, running to the general's side, "we tried to stop them."

"Damn!" General Wilson growled through clenched teeth. Frowning at the men around him, he shouted, "What the hell are you waiting for? Set those charges!"

"But sir, the boy and woman—"

General Wilson interrupted the lieutenant harshly, "We're just going to have to take that risk! There's no other way."

He walked away from Lieutenant Bryce and circled the pit. Three of the men were putting on safety harnesses while other troops hooked the harnesses to the winches.

Problems within problems, the general thought, his

head pounding with frustration. He understood the boy's concern for his parents, his desperation to find them, but David didn't seem to realize that they may be as good as dead already, that whatever the martians had done to them might be irreversible. Now the boy had only made things more complicated for him and his men.

General Wilson watched as the men walked to the center of the pit attached to the winches like puppets. They delicately set down brick after brick of explosives.

A tense silence settled around the pit as the men along the perimeter watched. . . .

The general started back around the pit toward Lieutenant Bryce, never taking his eyes from the men on the sand.

Moving gingerly, they set the last of the charges and turned, heading for the embankment. The still space of sand between them and the perimeter began to churn. They all lurched backward and began scrambling over the sand as the vortex opened up and began spinning toward them.

General Wilson saw with alarm that the cables were about to tangle above the heads of the three scattering men.

"Start the winches!" the general shouted, hurrying along the edge of the pit.

The winches cranked into action, pulling the demolition men off the sand, their feet dangling as the vortex swept violently beneath them. They were reeled in from the sand pit like fish from a lake.

But General Wilson was not entirely relieved. The churning vortex continued swirling across the pit toward the explosives.

"*Everybody back!*" he called, waving an arm.

The troops scattered for safety as the hissing whirlpool of sand swallowed the explosives, then smoothed over and disappeared.

After a brief, still moment, a column of sand rose from the pit toward the sky with an explosion so loud and powerful that General Wilson, huddling behind one of the assault vehicles, felt it rattle his eyeballs in their sockets. An instant later, a dry, gritty rainstorm of sand and tiny pebbles showered over them.

The men came from their cover slowly, a few at a time. General Wilson was the first to reach the edge of what had been the sand pit.

It was at least fifteen feet deep. The inside of the crater looked like a magnified cross section of an anthill. The charge had blown through two levels of caverns and tunnels that seemed to twist and snake in all directions. The walls were ridged, spiraled, and from somewhere in the complex structure, General Wilson could see an amber glow.

"But . . . where's the ship?" Lieutenant Bryce asked, confused, standing beside the general.

"Let's go find out. Bring some ladders!" General Wilson shouted, grabbing one of the cables and giving it a hard tug. Holding tight, he stepped over the edge and rappelled into the crater.

David's sleep was heavy, and rolled off him very . . . slowly. At first, he thought he was in a hospital; he thought he'd had his tonsils taken out again and was coming out of the anesthesia. But he was not on a hospital bed. He lay face down on a flat, hard, glasslike surface. Linda was lying beside him, unconscious.

David's voice cracked when he said, "Linda?"

Pushing himself up on his hands, he looked around. They were on a roughly oval-shaped slab, lying on the middle of three roundish, flat surfaces. David recognized the smell instantly—he was in the ship. There was a sound . . . a deep, whirring hum. . . .

Tugging on Linda's arm, David said quietly, "Hey, Linda."

Her arm was heavy; she was out cold.

The whirring grew louder.

David turned on his side, propped himself up on an elbow, and looked around. A few yards away on another table lay Captain Rinaldi, face down, motionless. Two bars of light hummed back and forth beneath him. They were bright and threw deep shadows of the captain all over the walls. Two drones flanked him, watching him carefully, waiting for a movement.

David looked up and held back a cry. Descending from a round orifice above was a long, needlelike device—it looked like a giant stinger! It slid from the aperture at a downward angle followed by a fat, lumpy base. It continued to descend until another fatter section was visible . . . then another . . . like a retractable telescope it continued to unfold from within itself. A pencil-thin beam of red light shined down on Captain Rinaldi's neck, pinpointing the exact spot at which the tip would land. As it got longer, descended further, David saw a luminescent drop of green fluid trembling precariously on the very end of the stinger.

That's where the cuts come from! David realized, standing.

Above the fleshy hypodermic device was the huge,

shimmering membrane he'd first seen in the central chamber. Behind it, David could make out a figure. A familiar figure—watching . . .

Mrs. McKeltch.

David's eyes swept back down to Rinaldi's neck as the long, glistening spike punctured the skin, sliding deep into the base of his brain.

We're next, he thought with a sickening lurch in his stomach.

"Linda!" David screamed, shaking her leg. "Linda, wake up!"

The drones turned their puffy eyes to him and rushed in his direction.

David darted around the operating table, still shouting, "Linda, please!" They were too close; he would have to run and leave her behind. He spun around and hurried through one of the wishbone-shaped archways. When he looked back, he saw one of them following him as the other turned back toward Linda. "Linda, wake up!" he screamed, his voice echoing hollowly through the passageway. "*Run,* Linda!"

He cut through a cloud of steam that had shot from one of the craters in the wall.

A drone lumbered out of one of the smaller side tunnels ahead and David found himself sandwiched between the two approaching creatures. He pressed on, trying to dodge the thing before him, but it reached out one of its long, powerful arms and grabbed him. Its flesh was thick and moist and the odor of it—a smell like rotting meat—clogged his nostrils as the creature pulled him into a deadly bear hug.

David opened his mouth to its limit and, with all his might, bit down on the creature's arm. His teeth broke through the sturdy flesh and warm fluid, green and thick, squirted from the wound, splashing his face.

The drone snapped its arm away from David and let loose a deafening roar of pain, like metal being crushed.

David ran, trying to keep from wretching at the horrible fluid on his lips and face. He wiped it away frantically. He could hear them following him, their heavy feet plodding on the ground. Two more drones stepped before him, their arms outstretched. David whirled around and screamed at what he saw.

One of the drones behind him was standing with its arms stretched open, as if to embrace him. Sliding from its middle, speeding through the air straight for David, was a long, fat tentacle. It moved so fast, David didn't have time to consider escape. It wrapped around his waist and squeezed tight. Lifting him off the ground a few feet, it began to retract, pulling David quickly toward the creature's waiting arms.

General Wilson and his men stormed down one of the tunnels, leaving the ladders behind for their escape. The general was alert to everything around him—the strange odor, the screwlike spiral of the tunnel—waiting for the slightest sound or movement.

"Incredible!" a voice behind him gasped.

He turned to see Dr. Feighan, one of the NASA scientists, examining the tunnel wall.

"God damn it!" the general blurted. "Only my men are to be down here!"

"But *look* at this!" the doctor marveled. "It's as if they . . . they *screwed* their way through the earth!"

"I don't have to be a *scientist* to see that!" General

Wilson snapped, stepping to the doctor's side and grabbing his arm. "But you have to be a *Marine* to be down here!" He turned to one of his men. "You! Take this man back up and keep him out of here!"

The Marine escorted the doctor back to the hole.

"Okay," the general called, "let's go."

They pressed on, guns at the ready. Their feet sounded like distant thunder.

At a bend in the tunnel ahead, General Wilson spotted a tall shadow approaching. He held up his hand. The men stopped and raised their guns.

Captain Rinaldi stepped around the corner and faced them.

"Rinaldi!" the general exclaimed. He smiled. At last, something good had happened. "We found you! What's—"

"Stop," Rinaldi said quietly. "Go back."

General Wilson felt the muscles of his face relax, then felt his shoulders fall.

Rinaldi took another step toward them. Shadows played over his gaunt, queasy face.

He was not the Captain Rinaldi who had been pulled into the sand earlier.

"Rinaldi, are you—"

"Go . . . back. . . ." He took a few more steps.

"Jesus," the general sighed, waving for one of his men to step forward.

Rinaldi didn't stop. He came closer and closer.

General Wilson nodded.

The man opened fire.

The bullets made Rinaldi dance and thrash. When he collapsed, lifeless, his uniform was darkening with blood.

General Wilson stepped forward and stood over his friend. A tendril of smoke rose from the dead man's neck as a needle slid out and sizzled. . . .

The drone lowered its tentacle, depositing David before the sluglike creature that rested on its throne. The drone had carried David high above its head through the tunnel and up a ramp. Its grip had been tight and when it let go, David took a deep, gasping breath of dank air.

The long, snaking creature was inches from David's face and he backed away from it, only to bump into the drone. The thing before him wheezed and hissed; its breath passed over David like a breeze from a garbage dump and he winced, turning his head and coughing.

When he turned, he spotted Mrs. McKeltch. She stood with her back to him, her hands locked just above her lumpy hips, staring through the opaque membrane.

David took a step toward her and was held back by the drone. From where he stood, he could see hazy images through the membrane, beyond Mrs. McKeltch. A limp figure was being secured to a table.

Linda!

"Let her go!" David shouted at Mrs. McKeltch.

She looked over her shoulder at him, then turned to him fully. Her lips squirmed into a satisfied smile.

"You're a very lucky boy, David Gardiner," she said. "Not everybody gets to meet the Supreme Martian Intelligence."

Slowly, David turned to the creature. It arched above him gracefully, hovering over the throne, the cilialike strands dangling below it. Wheezing like a fat man, it studied David. Muscles in its creased and flabby face twitched; its beady eyes blinked; its nostrils flared.

"Please . . ." David stepped toward it, searching his mind for the right words. "Please don't hurt Linda. Can't you just—"

"You've caused us a great deal of trouble already, David Gardiner," Mrs. McKeltch interrupted, walking toward him.

David ignored her. "Nobody did anything to you," he continued pleadingly, looking up at the Supreme Intelligence. "My mom and dad, Linda, all the others . . . they're good people. They never—"

"It's too late!" Mrs. McKeltch spat. "Too late."

David turned on her like an animal. "Shut up! I'm talking to him!" He turned to the creature again. "Please, can't you just—"

"It is too late, David Gardiner!"

He turned to her again, clenched his teeth, and growled, "Look, I'll stay after school every day for the rest of my *life* if you'll just shut . . . *up!*"

Her eyes widened and her lips parted in surprise.

To the Supreme Intelligence, he said, "Don't you understand? You can't do this to people! You can't control them like . . . like puppets! You're not gonna get away with this!"

Mrs. McKeltch stepped to his side and raised her hand above her head. *"One,* two, *three,* four, *five!"*

Ignoring her, he shouted at the beast, "You won't get away with it! We'll *stop* you!"

One of the tentacles wrapped around the throne slowly uncurled and raised above the creature, then whistled downward like a whip. It slammed David to the floor, face down.

The wind was sucked from David's lungs and a web

of pain spread over his back. Grunting, he turned his head to see Mrs. McKeltch's stubby black shoes inches from his face. He craned his head back just enough to look up at her face.

She was grinning as she hissed, "It's *your* turn now, David Gardiner."

The tentacle held him down firmly. He turned his face toward the Supreme Intelligence. Its mouth was curled into a sneer. The thin lips parted slowly to speak. The voice was a cold, mocking impersonation of Dad.

"Poor little guy," it said cruelly. "Poo-hoor little guy."

"No!" David screamed. He began kicking his legs and flailing his arms until he squirmed out from under the creature's tentacle. Crawling frantically, he got far enough away from the Supreme Intelligence to stand safely. He turned to the creature, saw its angry, piercing eyes, and David felt a rush of violence inside. He ran toward the Supreme Intelligence, ducking its whipping tentacle, and screamed. "I'll fix you, you . . . you *dick head!*"

David clenched his fist, pulled his arm back, and threw a punch with all his weight. His fist smacked between the creature's two flaring, wet nostrils and sunk into the flesh a bit.

Like a turtle pulling in its head, the Supreme Intelligence slid back into its aperture several feet, raising its head high above the throne, writhing its tentacles. Its eyes squeezed shut until they were lumps of taut muscle and its mouth opened; the roaring scream that came from it was David's idea of what it sounded like in hell.

The Supreme Intelligence continued to recoil; electric blue bolts of rampant energy raced around the chamber; sparks flew.

The drones staggered like drunkards, blinking with confusion.

Mrs. McKeltch pressed her hands to the sides of her neck and opened her mouth, but did not scream. She stumbled around silently, her mouth gaping.

The huge membrane sparked and fizzed.

David turned to run and heard Mrs. McKeltch moan, "*Nooo!*"

Her hand clamped onto his shoulder and pulled him back. Thinking fast, David reached over his shoulder into his backpack and grabbed his pouch of pennies. He spun around and held the pouch by its opening, swinging it hard. It struck Mrs. McKeltch in the temple and shattered. Pennies scattered everywhere and immediately began to sizzle and melt into the floor of the chamber.

Pennies! David thought, watching them disappear. *Copper! The ship uses copper! That's why they want it—for power!*

He stumbled backward as Mrs. McKeltch reached for him again. She staggered to her left, tripped, and fell on a bobbing, convulsing drone. It grabbed her blindly, lifting her off the ground. She began kicking her legs and opened her mouth to protest, but was silenced. The drone stuffed her into its cavernous mouth head first. Her legs hung out over the jagged fangs, kicking and kicking . . . until the drone snapped its jaws shut.

Blood spurted everywhere in a black-red shower as the drone tipped its head back and pulled her now limp body further into its mouth. . . .

David turned away and dashed toward the membrane, keeping a safe distance from the shooting sparks. Looking through it to the other side, he saw Linda lying face down on the table. The needle lowering slowly . . . closer and closer to her neck. . . .

Crossing the chamber quickly, David looked at the Supreme Intelligence again. It was painfully writhing its way back into its aperture, screaming all the way. The whole ship was affected, as if David had damaged a major organ. The drones stumbled and fell; energy bolts slammed dangerously around the chamber.

David ran down the ramp for all he was worth. . . .

Curtis and his men were still in the tunnels, trying to find their way into the ship. As they moved briskly toward yet another bend, Curtis thought he heard something.

"Halt!" he shouted, lifting a hand. "Listen!"

Somewhere in the winding tunnels he could hear a boy's voice: "Captain Curtis! General Wilson! Over here!"

"It's the boy!" Curtis shouted, taking off again, only to halt around the bend.

Two drones were startled by the Marines. One lifted its laser pod and fired. The beam struck one of the men and he was swallowed by flames, then gone without a sound.

"Get back!" Curtis shouted, waving. "Grenade," he said to a troop beside him.

The man pulled the pin on a grenade and threw it around the bend. They all moved back for cover.

Silence.

Curtis frowned when the explosion didn't come. Holding up his pistol, he stepped up to the corner and looked around it cautiously, just in time to see one of the drones plopping the grenade into its mouth.

The explosion threw a cascade of meat and green fluids over the tunnel walls.

When the smoke cleared, the men hurried on. . . .

David ran through the opening of the ship and into the tunnel. He'd heard gunfire and an explosion.

"Hey!" he shouted. "I'm here! Captain Curtis! General Wilson!"

His legs pumping like pistons, his knee pierced with pain, David shot around a corner and almost fell on his face trying to come to a stop.

Two drones.

They're all over the place! he thought.

One held a pod in one hand and a rectangular object in the other. The object seemed to be . . . of course! It was copper! The drone slipped the copper chunk into the back of the pod; it made a wet, sloshing sound. The drone aimed the pod at the wall. It opened up like a waking eye and a copper-colored beam shot into the wall. It made the tunnel wall glow, sizzle, and finally bubble as it melted away.

That's how they make those smaller tunnels, David realized, watching a hole form in the wall.

Suddenly there was an explosion of gunfire and David pulled his head back, then pressed himself against the wall as pieces of the drones flew through the air. Machine guns sputtered and men shouted and David nearly collapsed with relief.

The Marines had arrived!

When the gunfire stopped, David heard Captain Curtis's voice: "Jesus, I wasn't trained for *this!*"

He stepped around the corner and saw Curtis with General Wilson, backed by platoons of Marines.

"This way!" David shouted. "C'mon, *hurry!*"

They thundered into the central chamber, with David in the lead.

He saw the Supreme Intelligence looking at them, its eyes burning with hate. Tendrils of electricity were streaming down the walls of the chamber, fanning across the membrane.

Two of the men approached the throne of the Supreme Intelligence first, their guns aimed. A shimmering web of energy appeared around the throne and shot two bolts toward the men, piercing their chests. They collapsed, blackened and stiff.

The troops opened fire all at once.

Holes began to blossom in the face and body of the Supreme Intelligence as bullets ripped through its skin.

Screaming and flinching, the creature pulled back into its aperture rapidly, its tentacles slicing through the air. The round, flat panel slid over the opening, sealing off the creature.

The electrical activity subsided until only a few wild bolts shot around the walls.

"That thing!" General Wilson shouted, pointing to the membrane. "Blow it away!"

The men opened fire on the membrane.

David pressed his palms over his ears to keep out the roar of gunfire.

The membrane fizzed and sparked; smoke gushed from its edges; the opaque center tore away like skin, fraying around the ripped edges. Blinding flashes of light came from the rim of the membrane as it disintegrated under fire.

The shooting stopped.

The smell of gunfire stung David's nostrils. He dashed for the gaping hole and looked over the edge.

The long, cylindrical device was sputtering and shooting sparks. Its progress had been slowed, but it was still humming downward.

"Linda!" David screamed. He turned to the men, waved his arm, and shouted, "This way!" He led them down the ramp, around a corner, and into the operating room. "You've gotta stop it!" He pointed to the giant stinger descending toward Linda's neck.

"Get up there!" General Wilson shouted, waving three of the men forward.

They raised their guns and opened fire on the device.

Bullets riddled its fleshy surface and it jerked back, pulling into itself. Sparks showered down over the room and green fluid shot in every direction. It disappeared into its orifice.

Curtis hurried to Linda's side and David followed, weak with relief.

Linda stirred and began to sit up. Curtis slid an arm around her shoulders, supporting her.

"What's . . . what's going on?" she stuttered.

"Linda!" David breathed, near tears.

She opened her arms and he stepped into them. They held one another for several seconds as General Wilson began to give orders.

"Set some charges!" he shouted to the demolition men. "I want this blown to bits in five minutes!" He put a hand on David's head and said to Linda, "Are you all right, Miss Magnuson?"

She nodded, pulling away from David. "Yes," she said. "I'm fine. Can we . . . can we get out of here?"

"Right away." He turned to his men.

"I'm glad you're okay," David said.

She kissed his forehead and hugged him again, sitting up on the edge of the table. "Me, too."

The floor began to vibrate as a loud mechanical whine sounded from deep within the ship.

"What the hell is that?" General Wilson asked no one in particular.

David turned to him. "The engines!"

"Jesus! Everybody *out!*" To the demolition men, he said, "Charges set?"

"Yes, sir," one of them replied. "It'll blow in five minutes."

"C'mon!" the general called.

They hurried from the ominous room, down a short passageway, and through the archway. Once out of the ship, they ran through the tunnel, passing a fork, heading for the opening.

Linda saw it first and screamed.

Amber eyes burning, rotors spinning, the copper-colored router that had cut through the floor of the school basement earlier was speeding straight for them. . . .

Chapter Thirteen

"The fork!" David screamed. "Go back to the fork!"

David felt lost in the group of tall adults as they backtracked. He was jostled back and forth as he tried to keep from tripping over rushing feet. Linda held his arm tightly.

The router spun closer; the light from its eyes gave their skin and clothes a golden hue, darkening as it came closer.

They ducked around the bend into the other passage as the air churned around them violently, blowing their hair, fluttering Linda's skirt.

The creature's long, snakelike body was gone and its head shot freely through the tunnel. It folded its blades inward until it was a huge, veined ball. With a resonant slam, it flew into the entrance of the ship, plugging it like a cork in a bottle.

General Wilson stepped forward and looked skeptically at the motionless creature, waiting. . . .

"Sir," one of the men called.

"Yeah?"

"Less than four minutes before the charges detonate."

"Okay. Let's go."

The general raced several steps ahead of the rest of them toward the entrance; David was at his heels.

"Almost there, David," the general said without looking back at him. "Everything's gonna be just fine." General Wilson stopped in his tracks, looking up. "Bastards!"

David saw three cables—he recognized them as the cables used on the winches—hanging from above, and two ladders leading upward. But there was no opening.

"They've sealed off the entrance!" the general shouted angrily.

The cables and the ladders disappeared into the rounded ceiling.

"Two and a half minutes, sir!"

"Damn. Starting digging!" General Wilson ordered.

The men stepped forward and started digging like mad with their hands and the butts of their guns. But David knew it was hopeless. There was no way they could reach the surface before the explosion.

Linda squeezed his shoulders from behind. He turned and looked up at her puffy red eyes. She was crying; there was resignation in her face.

"There's gotta be a way out!" David hissed, looking desperately around the tunnel. It was entirely closed. David couldn't even find a crevice that opened to the outside.

He spotted something on the ground. Something oval-shaped . . .

"General!" David shouted, realizing it was a laser pod. He dashed forward and swept it into his hands.

The general and Curtis turned to David.

"I saw them digging with one of these!" David said. "It burns through the ground."

Curtis took the pod and examined it. There was an opening in the back; he tried to slip his hand in, but the opening was too small.

"Let me try!" David took the pod from Curtis. It was heavy and the surface was lumpy, like a gourd. He pressed his fingers together and slid his hand through the opening. The pod was wet inside and slippery; the walls seemed to tug at David's hand, pulling it in.

It's alive, he thought, wincing.

In the center, David curled his forefinger around what felt like a chicken bone.

"I think I found the trigger!"

Curtis put a hand on each side of the pod and aimed it at the wall, nodding for David to fire.

He pulled back on the trigger.

Nothing happened.

"Wait a sec. . . ." David found a slot on top of the pod, reached the thumb and forefinger of his free hand through the thick skin, and pulled out a black, charred rectangular object. "It was copper!" he said. "I saw them put it in. That's why they took my pennies—they want copper! For energy or something!"

"Maybe a penny would work," Curtis said.

"Shoot!" David stomped a foot. "I used to have a whole bag!"

"Who has a penny?" General Wilson roared, his face scrunched up, wrinkles cutting across his forehead.

The men began searching their pockets.

"Don't carry loose change into combat," one of them muttered.

"One minute fifteen seconds, sir!"

David closed his eyes as his dad's voice echoed softly in his memory: *Here, a fifty-eight-D in mint condition. I'll leave it for you here in your shirt pocket . . . shirt pocket. . . .*

"Here!" David yelped, fumbling his fingers into his shirt pocket. He found the penny in its small plastic case, pulled it out, and jabbed it into the slot. While Curtis held the pod, David squeezed.

The front of the pod opened with a sticky sound and the copper beam sliced into the wall. Dirt began to fall away. A large spot began to glow a burning red, then white, bubbling as it melted and spread. With a heavy thud, the spot fell away. Dirt and rocks crumbled out of the opening. Fresh air poured into the forty-five degree incline.

"Everybody out!" the general shouted, ushering David up through the hole.

"David . . ."

He stopped and turned at the familiar voice, stepping away from the hole to look back down the tunnel. Smoke was billowing from the direction of the ship. From the dirty white cloud emerged a figure, its arms outstretched.

"Mom!"

"David, come *on!*" Linda called as Captain Curtis helped her through the hole.

"In a second!" He started toward his mom, just as his dad stepped through the wall of smoke.

"Oh, David," Mom said, smiling.

"David, come with us." Dad held out a big, beckoning hand.

They came closer. . . . David stopped.

"Nooo," David groaned, moving back. They hadn't changed; their eyes were still blank and heavy. "No!"

They broke into a run as David turned and headed for the hole. The last of the men were crawling out, their backs to him. He ducked through the opening as his dad touched his arm.

"Come with us . . . *Champ.*"

"Noooo!" David wrestled his arm away and scurried up the hole. He could hear them behind him and feel Mom's hand slapping onto his foot for just an instant. "No, I won't come!" His voice was buried by the accelerating engines of the ship. They whined through the tunnel, tortured, mechanical voices echoing off the walls.

Through the mouth of the hole above, David could see the night sky; it was filled with bright stars and wispy clouds . . . and *freedom*. Freedom without his parents, he realized with horror. His chest burned with the certainty that tonight he would lose his mom and dad forever. . . .

He clutched the lip of the hole and pulled himself out.

Men were running everywhere; the winches and vehicles were abandoned as troops hurried for cover.

"Forty-five seconds!" one of them shouted.

"Everybody back!" General Wilson bellowed.

David crawled away from the hole, got his footing, and began to run. Everyone seemed to have forgotten him.

He looked back for an instant. His parents were little more than an arm's length behind him, and beyond them, he saw Doug! And Heather! And Mr.

Bob! Scot! Kevin! They were all emerging from the hole, their eyes on him.

Dad grabbed his backpack and David was jerked to a stop. Strong arms wrapped around his chest and lifted him off the ground.

"No!" David screamed. "No, please! Let me go!"

Dad turned and headed back for the hole as the ground beyond cracked. Great sections of earth were pushed upward and bars of light shined through the openings in the ground. The ship was rising.

David kicked and swung his arms futilely as he was rushed toward the ship.

It rose above the ground; dirt and rocks and roots slid from its glowing surface. Several feet up, it stopped and hovered with a deep, rumbling hum.

"They're waiting for you, David," Mom said with a smile—a cold, empty, dead smile.

"Lindaaaaa!" he screamed. "Help me!"

A ramp slid down from the ship as they drew closer; the others around them were heading for the opening.

They all drew back as an explosion blew a ragged hole in the side of the ship, spitting flames and sparks. Dad's grip loosened as he staggered back and David tore himself away.

Another explosion took out more of the ship and the ramp pulled up. David was knocked to the ground as the others began to fall and writhe, as if on fire. Dad grabbed his leg and pulled; David clawed his fingers into the dirt, trying to anchor himself.

With the third explosion, Dad let go and fell on his back, his legs kicking.

David stood, but could not run. He watched his parents and sobbed.

They clutched their necks, rolling on the ground, wretching, arching their backs, becoming rigid. . . .

"Mom!" he cried. "Dad!" He took a step back, another, but continued watching.

Linda's voice called his name in the distance as he backed away from them. Someone grabbed him from behind and he spun around. One of the Marines was pulling him to safety.

"C'mon, kid!"

"But . . . my . . . my mom and dad!"

A painfully loud blast came from the ship and the sky filled with copper light. David and the Marine fell to the ground.

The copper gave way to a bright white. David covered his eyes and screamed.

The light began to dim.

The ship's thrum became uneven and began to sputter weakly.

"Look!" the Marine shouted, getting to his feet.

David saw something spinning out of his dad's neck. It dropped to the ground and dirty smoke rose from it, sparks scattered, and then died.

He turned to his mom and saw the same thing. It lay beside her head, black and shriveled.

She opened her eyes.

Dad sat up, rubbing his neck.

"What . . . what's . . ." Mom's voice was hoarse and dry.

"Mom!" David shrieked. "Dad! Are you—" He crawled to them. "Are you all right?"

"David," Dad whispered, taking him into his arms, holding him tight.

Tears burned in David's eyes, cutting trails down his

dirty cheeks. He sobbed so hard, he felt his chest might explode.

"Oh, David . . ." Mom hugged him from behind.

The three of them huddled there, holding tight to one another as the entire ship exploded, its roar going on and on endlessly, setting the sky afire, blowing a hot and powerful wind over the ground that threw dirt in waves around them, burning their skin, blistering, tearing it away. . . .

Before David's horrified eyes, he saw his mom's face puff up with glistening blisters, watched her skin flake and blow away. He watched Dad's hair smoke and burn to an ashy white until he was bald, until his scalp began to burn away from the top of his skull. Their eyes flowed with tears, then blood that trickled in streams to their mouths which had been burned open farther and farther until their jaws were naked, shining bone. Their eyebrows disappeared and their eyeballs seemed to melt like butter, dribbling down their cheeks, mixing with the blood.

David screamed and reached a hand out to touch them, to help them somehow, and he saw the bones of his fingers sticking through charred skin, saw his flesh burning away until only his bare wristbone was left.

The ship continued to explode and burn and blow its fiery wind everywhere, howling like no wind had ever howled, mixing with the tortured cries of everyone around David, falling to their knees and wishing for death as their skin burned away like old paper.

"Maaaaawwwm!" David screamed. "Daaaaaad! Maaaawwwm! Daaaaad!"

Chapter Fourteen

"Maaaaawm! Daaaaad! Maaawwm! Daaaaad!"

"David! David, wake up! It's okay!"

"You're okay, Champ. C'mon, wake up, now."

He felt hands on his arms and shoulders, on his face, tangled blankets, sweaty pajamas.

David opened his eyes. First there was blurred darkness, then he made out faces . . . Mom and Dad. They loomed over him.

"No!" he screamed, horrified. "Leave me alone! Get away from me!"

"It's okay, Champ," Dad whispered, touching his face. "You're awake now. It's okay."

They were sitting on each side of him. Mom patted his chest; Dad stroked his hair with big, gentle hands.

David felt cold and trembly. His pajamas clung to his clammy skin and his lungs gulped air. When he tried to sit up, he found that he was so weak and shaky, he could do no more than squirm and fidget.

"Oooooh, shit," he sighed, trying hard to pull himself together and calm down.

Mom chided him gently, "David . . ."

He propped himself up on his elbows and looked around his room. Everything was fine. The comic books and magazines and toys were still scattered everywhere; none of them were broken or crushed. Light fell through the door from the hallway, stretching all the way across the messy floor to the window. Outside, David saw a gentle flash of lightning from far in the distance.

"Are you looking for something, honey?" Mom asked.

"No, it's just . . . well, they broke my stuff and stepped on things, and . . ."

"Who?" Dad asked.

Mom leaned forward, her hand still on his chest. "Who broke your things, hon?"

They really didn't know. It had all been a dream, every bit of it. But where had it started? Where had his waking hours ended and the dream begun? He couldn't be sure. . . .

"It was horrible," he said. "They chased me all over and they got you and Dad!" The memory clenched his throat and made his voice high and squeaky.

"They did?" Dad asked, cocking a brow.

"Calm down, honey," Mom whispered. "Just calm down." Her hand was warm and soft. "Now tell us . . . who chased you?"

"The mar—" He swallowed his words and searched their faces carefully.

Where had the dream begun? he wondered.

"Dad? Can I . . . let me look at the back of your neck."

"Boy," Dad chuckled. "It must've been a hell of a dream."

"Please, Dad . . . let me see."

"Okay, okay." He turned his head and pulled down his pajama collar.

David reluctantly touched his dad's neck. It was smooth and warm. No cuts, no bruises.

"Okay?" Dad asked.

"Yeah," David nodded, relieved. "Okay."

"Wait!" Mom sat up on the bed. "What about *me?*"

David felt so happy, he could only laugh. "You're fine, Mom."

"Phew!" she sighed with mock relief.

David lay back on his bed and told them the whole story, bouncing back and forth in the order of events as they faded in and out of his memory, some clear, some already crumbling

"That's pretty weird, David," Mom said when he was finished.

"Actually, I kinda liked the stuff about the martians coming to steal copper," Dad laughed. "Copper for energy, huh?"

David nodded. "It was so real."

Mom stood and went to his desk. "Well, look. Your penny collection is still here. You're okay. You've got nothing to worry about."

"You know," Dad said, "it sounds to me like your nightmare was made up of all sorts of things that happened to you today. The meteor shower . . . your penny collection . . . that big branch in the sand pit. Your mom said that Mrs. McKeltch was mad at you for being late. And Mad Dog Wilson came to your class today; I'm sure that had something to do with it." He smiled and shrugged. "That's what all dreams are. Just little pieces of things that happen to us. They fall together when we sleep and make one big, usually weird piece. That's all."

"Yeah, I guess so," David agreed. "But I was so scared."

Dad stood and went to the door. "You go back to sleep now, Champ. We can talk about it some more in the morning. You've got school. Love you." He walked out.

Mom went to the open doorway and turned to David. Her face was suddenly expressionless. When she spoke, an icy hand clutched David's heart.

"There is no need to be scared, David Gardiner," she said, her voice low and flat. "Tomorrow we will go for a picnic. On Copper Hill."

There was a scuffle in Jasper's terrarium. The lizard was rigid on its lump of bark; its mouth opened and it hissed loudly.

Mom stepped through the door and slammed it shut.

David whimpered, sitting up in bed. Was she joking? Or . . . Jasper *never* hissed unless he was angry or afraid. He'd never hissed at Mom before. Unless that wasn't Mom. . . .

With his next thought, David clapped his hands over his face and groaned with dread: *I didn't look at her neck!*

When David took his hands away and opened his eyes, spots of light were spinning on the walls. He sat up and looked over the foot of his bed. The planetarium was whirring around madly. David swung his legs from the bed and went to the window.

The floor beneath him began to vibrate; far in the distance he heard a familiar scream, hollow and metallic. He spotted movement deep in the night; something was coming closer very fast, screaming.

"No . . ." He took one step toward the door.

His window shattered; glass cut through the air and rain blew in as lightning flashed, illuminating the drooping face of the Supreme Intelligence, its mouth open, screaming . . . screaming. . . . Green fluid ran from the bullet holes in its face and its eyes opened wide as it shot straight toward David.

He screamed, heading for the door as the floor burst open. The air in his room swirled as the three-eyed router shot upward, its blades tossing aside large chunks of the floor and threw the bed against the wall with a thunderous clump.

He threw himself into the hall, screaming for his mom and dad as he ran for their room. He burst through the door and stumbled to a halt.

Their window was open. Rain was pouring inside. A drone turned to him, surprised. David recognized his father's leg in the drone's pincers; gnawed meat was visible through the torn pajamas. The creature was eating the leg like a drumstick. Mom was kneeling on the bed in a dark puddle of blood. She turned to David and smiled as the middle of the drone opened up and a tentacle shot toward him. The creature's mouth, bloody flesh clinging to its fangs, dropped open and it released a horrible, hawking cry. The tentacle wrapped around David and lifted him from the floor, pulling him straight into the drone's gaping jaws as he—

—sat up in bed with a throaty gasp. His eyes darted around the dark room. His heart was pounding against his ribs. Sweat ran down his forehead and temples, darkened his pajamas like blood, made his sheets sticky.

David held his head in his hands and whispered, "*What* . . . a *dream!*"

He threw the covers back and got out of bed, then hurried to the terrarium. Looking over the edge, he said, "Hey, Jasper. Are you okay?"

The lizard poked its head from under the bark.

David grabbed his shirt from the chair and reached into the pocket. The penny was still there, encased in plastic.

Wow, he thought, *a nightmare inside a nightmare!*

Hurrying to the window, he threw up the sash and leaned on the sill.

Storm clouds were gathering, but there were still enough breaks to see the meteor shower. Spots of light were still shooting across the black sky.

David smiled, covered his mouth, and giggled with giddy relief. He took a deep, cool breath of fresh air and exhaled slowly.

He suddenly frowned and cocked his head. . . . Was that . . .?

A distant hum.

Getting louder.

Louder still.

The windowsill began to vibrate beneath his hands. The panes began to rattle.

A heavy, dark thunderhead hovering over Copper Hill began to glow. Something very bright and very big slowly descended through the cloud cover. . . .

David backed away from the window. Tears welled in his eyes. "No," he muttered. "Please, not again."

He rubbed his eyes hard and fast with the heels of his hands.

It was still there.

"No, please let me wake up now . . . please, I want to wake up now. . . ."

It lowered beyond the hill.

"Not again. Wake up . . . please. . . ."

The light died. The sound stopped. The ship had landed.

"NOOOOOOOO!"

All these books are available at your local bookshop or newsagent, or can be ordered direct from the publisher.

To order direct from the publisher just tick the titles you want and fill in the form below.

Name ____

Address ______________________________________

____

Send to:
Panther Cash Sales
PO Box 11, Falmouth, Cornwall TR10 9EN.

Please enclose remittance to the value of the cover price plus:

UK 45p for the first book, 20p for the second book plus 14p per copy for each additional book ordered to a maximum charge of £1.63.

BFPO and Eire 45p for the first book, 20p for the second book plus 14p per copy for the next 7 books, thereafter 8p per book.

Overseas 75p for the first book and 21p for each additional book.

Panther Books reserve the right to show new retail prices on covers, which may differ from those previously advertised in the text or elsewhere.